Holiday

WeHo 2019 Holiday Edition

Sherryl D. Hancock

VULPINE
PRESS

Copyright © Sherryl D. Hancock 2020

All rights reserved. No part of this publication may be reproduced, stored in or introduced into a retrieval system or transmitted in any form or by any means, electronic, mechanical, photocopying, recording or otherwise without prior written permission from the publisher.

This is a work of fiction. Names, characters, places and incidents are either the product of the author's imagination or are used fictitiously, and any resemblance to any person or persons, living or dead, events or locales is entirely coincidental.

Published by Vulpine Press in the United Kingdom in 2020

ISBN: 978-1-83919-099-5

Cover by Claire Wood
Cover photo: Tirzah D. Hancock

www.vulpine-press.com

For my mother who always makes Christmas special! For Tirzah who makes every holiday and every day special. I love you both so much!

Also in the WeHo series:

When Love Wins
When Angels Fall
Break in the Storm
Turning Tables
Marking Time
Jet Blue
Water Under the Bridge
Vendetta
Gray Skies
Everything to Everyone
Lightning Strykes
In Plain Sight
Quid Pro Qup
For the Telling
Between Heaven and Hell
Taking Chances
Darkness Past
Stonewall Pride (special anniversary edition)
When All Else Fails
Out the Other Side

Chapter 1

Thanksgiving, 2019

"Bondye! This is madness!" Remi exclaimed as the doorbell rang for what seemed like the millionth time that afternoon.

"You were the one that suggest we have it here," Wynter reminded her girlfriend, giving her a humoring wink.

Remi threw up her hands as she headed out of the kitchen to answer the door. Wynter watched her go with a grin on her lips. The fact was their house was one of the larger ones in the group and it would accommodate everyone coming that day, which was basically the whole group. They'd bought a house in the Hollywood Hills, right under the Hollywood sign. The house sat on a lot which was three quarters of an acre and boasted 4,500 square feet with an open floor plan and walnut floors throughout. The "yard" was partly decked and had a large pool with a green area off to the side and expansive views of Los Angeles and the ocean. The price tag befitted the large, beautiful home, but between Remi's sale of her New York place and Wynter's sale of her house in West Hollywood, they'd been able to make a substantial down payment on the 7.5-million-dollar home.

The home's media room would keep what Remi liked to call "the kids" entertained—set with an 85-inch Samsung gaming TV with all the bells and whistles. They'd hooked up both a PlayStation 4, and an Xbox to the home theater system and TV. They'd told their friends to bring any game they wanted to play. Harley, Jet, Cody, Dakota, and one of their newest friends Sydney would likely spend most of the day and evening heavily entrenched in playing.

Around the rest of the house they'd set various areas for smaller groups to gather and talk. Dinner was being prepared by the "moms" of the group, including Wynter, Ashley, Sierra, Savannah, and Riley, and they had been working since early that morning.

The bois had turned out in force that morning to help set up a tent in the backyard with tables and chairs for everyone. Remi, Kai, Rayden, Kashena, Jericho, Lyric, and honorary "boi" Sebastian had worked tirelessly setting things up to allow for comfortable dining. They noted that it was a good thing the temperatures in Los Angeles were expected to be a balmy seventy-five degrees for late November.

"We'd never have fit everyone in the dining room, no matter how big it is!" Wynter had exclaimed.

With around fifty friends coming to share the meal with them, things were bound to get crowded quickly! As it was cars would fill their vast driveway and the drive leading to the house; at least they didn't have to contend with West Hollywood parking which was nearly impossible most days.

As people arrived, Remi did her best not to regret her suggestion that people come to their house. Wynter had assured her that they'd hire a cleaning service to clean up the mess the following day while they were resting. Legend arrived with Parker and Talon, who'd brought Parker's granddaughter Ginny with them. The two-year-old promptly toddled off to play with Anastasia, Lyric and Savanna's two-and-a-half-year-old daughter. They were playing with the Frozen tea set that Anastasia had gotten from her sister, Dakota, the day before.

"Kim didn't come?" Wynter asked, having invited Parker's daughter to Thanksgiving as well.

"No, she has to work tonight." Parker shook her head, grinning. "But she said she'd love some leftovers."

"There should be plenty," Quinn muttered, rolling her eyes at the massive amount of food the women were preparing.

"Quiet, you!" Xandy told her wife, flicking her on the ear. They'd been married the month before and were still looking for their first home together.

"Just tell me we don't have to buy a house like this," Quinn commented, gesturing to the massive space around them.

"No..." Xandy pouted slightly. "But I want something nice..."

Quinn looked immediately contrite. "We'll buy whatever you want," she assured her new bride and then promptly gave her friends a vile look as chiding rounds of "aww" began. "Shut up, all of you!"

When Harley and Shiloh arrived, Cody, McKenna, Dakota, and Jazmine weren't far behind. Quickly followed by painfully shy Sydney with her girlfriend Mia. Remi showed them to the media room, where Harley and Sydney promptly *oohed* and *aahed* over the gaming TV.

"Dude! This is a 4K! I need one of these!" Sydney exclaimed, forgetting she was in the presence of a stranger. Mia and Shiloh exchanged a grin, happy that Sydney was becoming more and more comfortable with the group. Sydney had been extremely worried about the huge crowd that day.

Shiloh nudged Harley slightly. Harley, who was busy examining the setup, jumped a little, but knew what Shiloh was indicating. "Oh! Yeah, it's got a quantum processor, so it's hella fast on the reload!"

"Look what I brought!" Cody taunted, holding up the very latest zombie fighting video game on the market.

"Gimme!" Dakota grabbed, laughing as she did.

Remington watched as the two computer nuts devolved into an entire discussion about RAM speed and a lot of other jargon she didn't understand. And Dakota and Cody continued to play 'keep away' with the game. Leaning in, Remi told Shiloh, Mia, McKenna, and Jazmine, "There's fortification in the other room, ladies, if either of you are of the mind."

"I'm on that!" Mia agreed immediately.

"Me too," Shiloh said, putting a finger up in another vote.

"I'm in," McKenna said, shaking her head as her wife bowled over one of the gaming chairs trying to keep possession of the gaming disc.

"Gimme!" Jazmine crowed, as she rolled her eyes at Cody and Dakota's antics.

Remi escorted the four ladies from the room, throwing glances over her shoulder at "the kids." She led them straight to the fully stocked wet bar next to the living room.

"This is some view," McKenna said as she looked out the floor to ceiling windows that led to the outer deck. "You can see all the way down to the ocean from here!"

"It is nice," Remi agreed.

"You two did an amazing job finding this house!" Jazmine exclaimed.

Remi, always the humble one, merely inclined her head.

"They're under the fecking Hollywood sign!" Quinn laughed, clapping Remi on the shoulder.

"I can give you our realtor's card," Remi commented drolly.

"Bite your damned tongue!" Quinn growled, causing raucous laughter from the girls.

"Oh stop," Zoey, who had just walked in with Jovina and Catalina, stated, putting her hand on Quinn's arm as she leaned in to give the Irishwoman a kiss on the cheek. "You'll buy your wife anything she asks for."

"Even if it's made out of gingerbread." Cat winked at Quinn as she needled her too.

"I can't believe I invited you people to my wedding!" Quinn huffed, despite the humorous twinkle in her eye.

"Men, out te fè," Remi said as she put her arm around Quinn's shoulders. "Yet you did," she translated.

"What did she do this time?" Kai queried from the living room. She set down the case of wine she'd carried into the house, causing more rounds of laughter, even as Remi shook her head at her friend and former trainer.

"Where's your girl?" Wynter asked Kai, as she began taking bottles out of the box to hand off to Savannah to put in the industrial-sized fridge.

"At the hospital, where else?" Kai shrugged. "She'll be along, don't worry. She was headed into an emergency appendectomy when I talked to her an hour ago."

"Better someone else, than you," Remi put in, as she came up to shake hands with Kai in welcome.

"Damned skippy," Kai said, remembering well the way she and Finley had met.

"And Cass?"

"She's here. She and Erin are thick as thieves. They're talking about their classes and finals," she added proudly.

"They're both at UCLA, right?" Wynter asked.

Kai nodded. "Yes, and both doing well."

"And still a couple, huh?" Remi asked.

"As far as we can all tell." Kai chuckled.

"Oh, they are." Quinn nodded. "Erin is forever talking my ear off about Cassiana, saying how much more mature she is than a nineteen-year-old would normally be. Like she's trying to justify being with someone two years younger." Quinn rolled her eyes.

"Years mean a lot to them at this age," Lyric put in as she reached for a bottle of wine. Wynter handed her an opener without a word.

"Says the wise mother of three," Savanna put in from the kitchen, winking at her wife.

"Speaking of mothers, are Ty and Shenin here yet?" Riley asked. "I'm just dying to get my hands on that baby!"

"Easy, babe…" Legend cautioned, "the kid's only like, what, three months?"

"Seven months tomorrow," Tyler commented as she walked up holding Aiden.

"Gimme, gimme!" Riley gestured, holding her hands out.

Tyler dutifully handed her son over, knowing that he would get handed around a lot this particular day. Shenin and she had discussed it at length before accepting the invitation. Because Shenin was breastfeeding, the doctor had told them that it would likely be okay for Aiden to be at a large gathering at his age. "He's a healthy little guy," the doctor had told them the week before at his checkup.

As Riley cuddled the blond baby, she shot her daughter-in-law a look. "When are you and my daughter going to give me a grandchild?"

"We still need to get married," Kai informed Riley.

"And when will that be?" Wynter asked.

"Right after you and Remi," Kai shot back with a twinkle in her eyes, as she poked at Remi.

"Manyen," Remi replied, saying "touché" in Creole.

"Ty, did he…? Oh!" Shenin pulled up short as she approached and noticed that her son was now in Riley's arms. "I was going to ask if he needed changing." Shenin grinned.

"Oh, I'll do it!" Riley enthused.

"I'll help!" River said, having been trying to assist in the kitchen since she and Sinclair had arrived.

"Sinclair, your girl's going all gooey eyed over a baby!" Quinn called to the blonde.

Xandy swatted Quinn on the butt. "Quit being a tattletale."

Sebastian walked up with his son in his arms. At three and a half, Benjamin Bach was the only boy in the group of younger children. Benjamin was sniffling from what had obviously been a crying jag.

"What happened, baby?" Ashley asked Benjamin, who only pouted.

"He's decided he doesn't like Frozen." Sebastian chuckled, as Ashely took their son.

"But you liked Olaf," Ashley told the boy.

"Just give Aiden time," Tyler told the little boy. "He'll be playing trucks with you before you know it!"

Benjamin brightened at that thought.

"C'mon," Quinn said, holding her hand out to the boy, "we'll go watch the bois play video games." She cast a stink eye at the group at large. "It's getting way too aggressive in here for me."

The group laughed as Quinn walked off with Benjamin.

"Did Jet get here yet?" Wynter asked the room. "She was bringing beer."

Remi looked around them and spied cases of beer near the front door. "Looks like she's here; the beer's here."

"I'd put a twenty on her being in the game room with the kids," Skyler said as she and Devin walked into the kitchen. "I'll help Remi get the beer."

"That ADHD little shit…" Devin muttered as she shook her head. Jet was well known for being forgetful. She wasn't as hyper-focused as Harley tended to be, and she could forget things easily in the face of fun.

"I'll help," Sebastian said, grabbing Rayden and Jericho as he walked by them.

Jet had indeed shown up with multiple cases of beer. Many of them were still outside the front door. Fadiyah had told them that she tried to keep Jet on track, but the sound of the gaming in the other room had been too much.

"This is why we don't need children," Fadiyah told the group as she took a glass of wine from Savanna gratefully.

"Who doesn't need children?" Kashena asked as she brought in a case of beer. "I got caught by the beer brigade."

"Jet," Shiloh put in, taking another glass of wine.

"Oh yeah, that's true," Kashena agreed.

"Don't be judgmental," Sierra warned her wife.

"What?" Kashena replied defensively. "I love Jet, but she's still a child, she doesn't need to have any yet. I feel sorry for Fadi."

"Blessings on your house," Fadiyah replied, lifting her glass to Kashena, making everyone chuckle. Fadiyah had been fitting into the group more and more over the past three years. Everyone had come to not only love Jet's young bride, but also to feel a bit sorry for her having to try and handle Jet and her rambunctious ways.

"Did Colby come with you two?" Wynter asked, still trying to tally all of the people she had to feed, terrified there wouldn't be enough food.

"No," Sierra said, shaking her head, "he had other plans."

"What he had," Kashena said, taking a beer from Sebastian, "is a new girlfriend and parents who invited him to their Thanksgiving." Her ire at her son was evident in her voice.

"It's okay," Sierra said.

"It's not, babe, he should be with his family on Thanksgiving," Kashena argued. It was clear to everyone that this had been a bone of contention for a bit.

Sierra drew in a deep breath. "I know you think that, and I appreciate it, but he's got to make his own choices. I'm not going to force him to do what he clearly doesn't want to do, that would make me just as bad as…"

"You aren't as bad as Jason, Jesus!" Kashena raged, then suddenly remembered where they were, and looked around at the group. "And that's what I get for marrying a lawyer. She can argue both sides of every point." She sighed.

"She's right, though," Sinclair put in. "I was dragged to so many things as a kid, and I ended up resenting never getting to make my own choices."

"See?" Sierra soothed, touching Kashena on the cheek. "It's one holiday, love."

"I think Kash needs a serious drink," Gun offered as she, Sable, Gage, and Kit walked in.

"You made it!" Kashena exclaimed, hugging Gage, Sable, and Kit, and shaking hands with Gun.

"Having a private jet at your disposal is handy." Gun winked, leaning in to kiss Sable. They'd been up in San Francisco scouting for houses to buy in the Castro. After the events of the summer it had been decided that OES needed two offices, and Gage had asked Gun to head that office.

"Living the life, huh?" Sebastian asked, shaking Gun's hand as well.

"Might as well," Gun said.

"Right, 'cause you're not living it up heading back to San Fran!" Gage told her friend.

"She loves it, don't let her tell you different." Sable smiled, just as she spotted Cat and Jovina. "Excuse me."

Sable made her way over to the other couple. She was happy when Cat immediately opened her arms to hug her.

"Congratulations!" Cat said to Sable. "You look very happy."

Sable hugged Cat back, nodding as she did. "I am, thank you." She extended her hand to Jovina. "How are you?"

"I'm good," Jovina said, nodding. "Congratulations on your engagement."

"Thank you." Sable inclined her head. She glanced around them, and out the window at the setting sun. "Wow, some view, huh?"

"It's incredible!" Cat agreed. "We're hoping to buy something here soon."

Sable nodded, realizing suddenly that it didn't hurt to talk to Catalina about her plans with her girlfriend anymore. Falling in love with Gun had been absolute.

"You know if I can help..." Sable began, seeing Cat grin and shake her head.

"No, no," Cat told her, remembering well the Porsche Cayenne SUV incident, where Sable bought Cat an SUV to replace one that was totaled, surprising her with the vehicle. "We got this. Jovi's handling scripts for Legend's movies these days, so she's doing pretty well."

"Not *this* well," Jovina put in, with a gesture to the house around them and a smile, "but better than before."

"Oh, that's right, I'd heard that. It's is bloody fantastic!" Sable enthused. It was a comfortable conversation and it made Sable's heart happy.

"She's doing fine," Gage told Gun as they watched the conversation between Sable, Cat, and Jovina.

"Yes, she is," Gun said, having been watching to see if she needed to rescue her fiancée. "Kash, let's get that drink."

As Kashena and Gun walked away together, Sebastian grinned. "I guess she was worried about a 'Cat-fight,'" he said with his usual sense of humor.

"Hardy har." Kashena rolled her eyes at her long-time partner and friend.

"Everything okay?" Memphis asked from behind them, her eyes on Sable and Cat, a hint of concern in her voice.

"Everything is fine," Kashena assured the younger woman. Memphis was remembering the fight between Gun and Cat at the bar months before and was worried something would break out between Sable and Cat. She liked everything calm. "How are you two?" Kashena asked, smiling at Kieran.

"We're lovely," Kieran told Kashena, smiling brightly, putting her head against Memphis's shoulder.

"What are you working on these days?" Sierra asked the young DJ and brilliant sound engineer.

"She's been lent to me again," Legend said, walking up and hugging Memphis around the shoulder. "Just a short project, some music for my next movie."

"Engineering or singing?" Sebastian asked.

"Engineering!" Memphis answered quickly. "Gods yes, engineering, no more singing."

The small group gathered around Memphis and Kieran widened their eyes, having caught the near fear in Memphis' voice.

"Is BJ pressuring you to make another album?" Xandy asked as she went to get more wine.

"Yes, he is," Kieran told Xandy.

"That man, I tell you…" Xandy shook her head. "He thinks everyone wants to be a star."

"I don't," Memphis said simply, looking nervous.

"And he's not going to make you," Remington told her young friend as she hugged Memphis hello.

Memphis stayed in Remi's arms for a long moment, like she was taking shelter there. It was obvious BJ Sparks had been pressuring the young woman. Eyes narrowed all around.

"What's up?" Quinn asked, having come back from leaving Benjamin with the bois.

"Apparently BJ is pushing Memphis to do another album," Xandy told Quinn.

"That true?" Quinn asked Memphis.

Memphis nodded, having stepped out of Remi's arms.

"Feck that! I'll flatten him!" Quinn exclaimed.

There were grins on every face in the area. Quinn was fiercely loyal to her friends and thought of Memphis like she did her little sisters.

"Did you ever tell him you didn't want to make more albums?" Quinn queried.

Memphis looked a bit sheepish in response, and Quinn rolled her eyes, shaking her head. "We'll deal with him."

"Alright everyone, time for dinner!" Wynter announced. "Put down your pitchforks and torches and grab a plate!" She winked at Remi as she said it.

Remi laughed, and led Memphis over to the large island in the kitchen. "You need to eat, you're too skinny, little one!"

A half an hour later, there were toasts for Thanksgiving, and good friends and family to share a meal with. There was tons of food: a turkey, ham and a full prime rib, many different side dishes for everyone's tastes, as well as a few dishes from various members of the group. Fadiyah had made an Iraqi dish called Quzi, which was roasted lamb stuffed with aromatic rice, vegetables, and nuts. Xandy had learned to make Irish Brown Bread from Quinn's mother and had made a few loaves to go with the meal. Legend had contributed an Israeli salad her mother used to make with cubed tomatoes, cucumbers, yellow bell peppers bathed in a light olive oil, lemon juice dressing, with sprigs of fresh rosemary. It was definitely an international meal as well traditional.

Everyone was eating and enjoying their meal, and various conversations went on at the tables. At one table, Shenin sat breastfeeding Aiden, an Air Force blanket covering her modestly, with Tyler sat next to her, feeding her bites of her dinner. Savanna, Lyric and Anastasia were sitting at the same table, along with Cody, McKenna, Dakota, Jazmine, Jet, and Fadiyah.

"He is so friggin' cute!" Cody said, not for the first time that evening.

"Are you two planning on kids?" Shenin asked, glancing between Cody and McKenna.

"I don't know," Cody answered, looking over at her wife. "Are we?"

McKenna raised an eyebrow. "Would you be able to handle a baby?"

Lyric laughed. "She has a valid point."

"Thanks, Mom!" Cody remarked sourly.

"You like your freedom, honey. It's not a bad thing," Savanna soothed.

Cody canted her head, looking at her little sister, watching as Anastasia pulled the crust off her bread daintily. "I do alright with Annie."

"'Cause you're not with her twenty-four seven," Lyric informed her.

"Well, why don't you guys leave her with me and Kenna while you go on your little camping trip?" Cody huffed.

"Camping trip?" Tyler perked up. "Where are you going?"

"We're shooting for Yosemite," Lyric said, seeing Savanna roll her eyes. "Stop it."

"Uh?" Tyler looked between the two quizzically.

"One of the guys at the department is selling his rig and camper, and he's letting us try it out before we buy it. Savanna is being a hater."

"I'm being realistic, what do you know about camping?" Savanna asked.

"Camping is awesome," Tyler put in, her face lit with excitement. "My family used to tent camp over on the Potomac at Westmoreland State Park every year. I loved it!"

"Maybe you and Shenin should come," Lyric put in.

"With a baby?" Shenin asked incredulously.

"We used to take babies all the time in my family," Tyler countered, looking even more excited by the idea.

"With the size of your family you didn't have a choice." Shenin grinned. "We don't own a tent."

"You could stay in the camper with us," Lyric said as she warmed to the idea, enjoying the thought. "Hell, we could see if anyone else wants to come."

"The camper isn't that big," Savanna told her wife sourly.

"It's definitely big enough for Shenin, Ty, and Aiden," Lyric replied.

"I don't know…" Shenin said. "Aiden's up at all hours of the night still, I wouldn't want to ruin your trip."

"There's actually a whole room of its own in the back of the camper. You'd have a door and everything," Lyric said.

"That would be so fun!" Tyler said. "I've never been to Yosemite before."

"When are you going?" Shenin asked.

"Next week—we're going for ten days. Since it takes like seven or so hours to get there in a car, I figure the camper will take a bit longer," Lyric said.

"I think I'd like to do a tent camp," Tyler said. "We could buy some stuff, Shen."

"It's fall, babe," Shenin said, to Tyler, "it's gonna be cold up there. If the roads are even open."

"It's seventy-five degrees today, there's no rain in the forecast for the next two weeks! Not even up north!" Tyler was practically pleading now. Shenin knew they needed a bit of a break, work had been crazy, with setting up new offices. Tyler had been helping out now that she was retired from the military.

It would be nice to get away… Shenin thought wistfully.

"I suppose we could, as long as we bring the right things for Aiden. If you're sure you won't mind," Shenin said, putting her hand over Savanna's on the table.

"You're more than welcome," Savanna said, smiling.

"Any chance we could join you?" Jet asked from the other side of the table, glancing over at Fadiyah as she did.

"The more the merrier!" Lyric exclaimed.

"I think we'd do the tent camping. I used to camp up in Washington, but Fadi's never been camping. I want her to experience it the right way."

"I think it would be fun," Fadiyah agreed, smiling brightly.

"Well there you go."

The discussions ensued about who would bring what, and before long Quinn wandered by, and not only indicated her interest in joining, but also got Jericho and Zoey involved.

"I've been dying to check out Yosemite," Zoey said. "We could even check out Bodie if you guys were interested. It's an old ghost town about an hour and a half from Yosemite—it's supposed to be really cool."

"That does sound cool!" Xandy said, having never been anywhere like that in California.

"Sounds like a party!" Quinn pronounced.

***

"You're going to be gone how bloody long?" BJ asked, doing his best not to growl. The idea of his star being gone "camping" before a European tour didn't exactly thrill him.

"Ten days," Xandy told him, not for the first time, doing her best not tremble as she did. BJ still scared the hell out of her.

"And you're going hiking in the bloody forest?" BJ snapped.

"Yes," Xandy answered, like a witness giving no more or no less of an answer.

BJ's blue-green eyes narrowed slightly; he knew Quinn had everything to do with this. "If you break something…" he threatened.

"I'll go on the tour anyway, maybe I'll garner the sympathy vote," Xandy put in, feeling suddenly like a mischievous child.

"Whatever you break, I'll break the other one, and don't make me tell you what I'll do to Cavanaugh," BJ raged, even as a grin started on his lips. He knew he had no right to tell Xandy she couldn't go, and Xandy Blue was probably one of the easiest artists he worked with, so he didn't have the heart to bully her into not going. He gave a long-suffering sigh, then leaned over his expansive desk, designed that way to intimidate artists and managers on the other side of it, and patted her hands that were folded primly on the mahogany wood. "Have a good time. Just come back in one piece please."

"I'll do my very best," Xandy said, breathing an inner sigh of relief. She'd been dreading telling him since Thanksgiving, and it had taken until the day before the trip to get a meeting with him. She knew she still had a few promotional appearances to do before the tour, and she'd been terrified he'd tell her she couldn't go because of them. Who ever heard of starting a tour the day after Christmas anyway?

As she left his office she called Quinn to let her know that BJ had approved. "Good, now I don't have to kick his ass for two things!" was Quinn's response.

Quinn had been brooding about BJ's badgering of Memphis about another album, and really wanted to confront him about it. Xandy had begged her not to, at least until after the tour, because she was afraid BJ would do something drastic like cancel it. Xandy didn't want that; she did, however, wish the tour could wait, but apparently she and Wynter were set to appear in London on New Year's Eve, so that wasn't happening.

***

"Are you going to make it home in time?" Fadiyah asked Jet on the phone. It was the day before the trip and Jet had been called to Washington, D.C. two days earlier for some critical translation they needed.

"Yeah, I'll make it," Jet said, as she walked through the FBI building. "I've already given them what they needed, I just need to get back to the airport and grab a flight."

"Would you like me to start packing for you? We leave tomorrow," Fadiyah asked, eyeing Jet's side of the closet, already trying to determine what to bring.

"Sure, just grab stuff that'll be warm. Probably a few pairs of jeans, and my black hiking boots if you can find them," Jet said, rolling her eyes as she realized she had no idea where those had ended up. She'd expected to have time to pack properly and find or buy what she needed. Now time was tight. "Just do your best, babe, I'll get home as fast as I can."

"I will do my best." Fadiyah smiled, knowing that Jet always left things until the last minute. It was her way of doing everything. "Alsafar amna," she said, telling Jet to travel safely in Arabic.

"I will, love you."

"I love you as well," Fadiyah responded softly.

"Arak lahaka."

"I will see you soon too." Fadiyah smiled warmly. It always warmed her heart that Jet not only spoke her language, but did it so very well with a perfect accent.

Jet had learned more Arabic in the three years they'd been married. She was always asking Fadiyah how to say something

18

"properly." It spoke volumes about Jet's dedication to her, and Fadiyah felt very lucky to have found this wonderful person to love.

The airport at Reagan International was insane. By the time Jet got through security and checked for flights, she had to wait for three hours. She finally flew out at 10 p.m. and had a two-hour layover in Denver that got extended due to snow. She finally walked through the door at 3 a.m. the next morning. She immediately started to pack her 67 black Mustang with their gear.

"Are you sure you want to go on this trip?" Fadiyah worried as she watched Jet working.

"Of course!" Jet told her. "I got some sleep on the plane, I'm okay!"

"But Jet…" Fadiyah began. "They'll be here by six, you won't have a chance to sleep anymore."

"I'm fine, babe, really!" Jet told her.

***

"I'm still here," Lyric told Savanna. It was 8 p.m. the day before their trip. She'd planned on taking the day off, but one of the cases she was managing had gone sideways, and she'd spent all day mopping up. "Did you get the stuff in the camper?"

"I've put everything in that I can at this point. We'll need to load the coolers and stuff in the morning before we head out," Savanna said, eyeing the two coolers sitting near the refrigerator. "We're going to have to run out and get ice on the way, I guess…"

"I'm sorry, babe, this wasn't how I expected it to go," Lyric said, hearing that Savanna sounded tired. "Trust me, you'll get a chance to rest tomorrow on the drive. Just think, no Anastasia asking a million questions!" There was silence on the other end of the line, and Lyric knew that Savanna was frowning. "Babe, we talked about this…" she began.

"I know!" Savanna exclaimed. "But that doesn't mean I have to like it."

"It'll give Code and Kenna a good opportunity to see what a toddler is like twenty-four seven. It'll be good for them and give us a bit of a break too."

Savanna sighed heavily. "I know… I just… what if something happens?"

"Babe, we've talked about this over and over. Cody knows first aid, CPR, and Finley is on speed dial. It will be fine!"

"I know, I just worry, you know that," Savanna admitted.

"Yes, I know." Lyric grinned on her end, then saw one of her people signal her. "I gotta go, babe, I love you! Try to get some rest. I'll be home as fast as I can."

"Be careful," Savanna said.

"I will, I love you."

"Love you."

They hung up then. Lyric walked through the front doors of their home at midnight.

***

"Is everything going to fit?" Xandy asked as she brought out another bag.

"It would if ya'd stop bringing stuff out," Quinn muttered and was promptly bonked on the butt with the bag Xandy was holding.

"Excuse me, these are your clothes!" Xandy told her blithely. "I can go put them back if you want me to…" With that Xandy started to walk away with the bag.

"Get back here, girlie!" Quinn laughed as she grabbed Xandy around the waist, taking the bag out of her hands and snuggling her as she did. "What else is left?" she asked after a few long kisses.

"Umm, sleeping bags, and I think that blow-up mattress thingy."

Quinn surveyed the trunk of the Charger. She'd chosen the Charger due to its larger trunk, but it had filled up quickly. "I think we're gonna have to put that stuff in the back seat."

"Why do you say that like you really don't want to?" Xandy queried.

"'Cause I don't want some arsehole breakin' my windows to get at a sleeping bag. Those windows are a pain to find, and expensive to boot."

"And it would hurt one of your babies," Xandy commented knowingly.

Quinn pressed her lips together in a grim smile. "And that."

Xandy nodded. "Well, is there anything we can skip?"

"Probably, but I'd have to unload the whole trunk, and they'll be here any minute," Quinn said, looking at her watch. "We'll just put it in the back, and hope no one is stupid enough to risk their life." Quinn's wicked grin made Xandy smile.

Quinn was definitely tough enough to take on just about anyone, but Xandy loved the woman more than life itself. She loved that she got to see the soft side of Quinn Kavanaugh, a part many people never did. It made Xandy feel much more special to be married to the tough-as-nails Irishwoman.

As if on cue, the large Ram truck towing a camper came around the corner right as Quinn closed the back door to the Charger. Behind the camper came a blue Dodge Challenger, a red Challenger Hellcat, and Jet's flat black Mustang.

"Ready to go?" Lyric asked from the truck.

"Yup!" Quinn called, opening the passenger door for Xandy, then going into the house to set the alarm and make sure doors were locked. A minute later she came back out and started the classic Charger with a satisfying roar.

Lyric and Savanna exchanged a grin. It had already been a morning, packing up the last of the stuff for the camper whilst chasing Anastasia down to put her in her car seat in the truck to drop her off at Cody and McKenna's. Lyric thanked her lucky stars that Anastasia loved being with her big sister and McKenna. Dakota and Jazmine had also promised to help them out. There were no tears from the baby when they left, but that couldn't be said for her mother. Savanna had cried for ten minutes on the way over to Jet's house. Lyric felt bad, but she also knew that what they were doing was for the best. The trip would probably be hard on the three-year-old, and they had no idea what they were doing just yet. Lyric wanted to be better at "camping" before she took their daughter with them.

Everyone had a map and directions to their first stop, in Bakersfield, to have breakfast and gas up. Each car had a walkie talkie and they'd already set their channels. As they headed out, they ran into the usual Los Angeles traffic—it took an extra forty-five minutes just to get out onto the freeway. That's when the fun began.

Chapter 2

"You aren't going to be able to keep up with her…" Shenin said to Tyler. In response, Tyler pressed harder on the gas pedal of Shenin's Challenger. Shenin glanced at the mirror set up on their son in the back seat. He was in his rear-facing car seat, but Tyler had insisted that she needed to be able to see Aiden at all times, so had installed the mirror and angled it so she could. "Your mommy is crazy," Shenin told Aiden, "she thinks she's going to catch a Challenger Hellcat with my little old regular Challenger…"

"Ya know…" Tyler commented, curling up her nose at Shenin.

"What, babe? I couldn't afford a Hellcat on an airman's salary."

"You haven't been an airman for a long time, babe… Maybe it's time to trade up."

"Maybe you shouldn't insult the car that's transporting you at this time," Shenin chimed in.

Tyler stared into the review mirror, catching a look at their son. "You hear that? Mommy doesn't want a tougher car… She likes getting her butt kicked by some non-comm."

Shenin chuckled, shaking her head and patting the dashboard. "Don't listen to her, baby, she's just a hater."

"And so it begins…" Quinn muttered to herself as she pressed harder on the gas, shooting past Jet's Mustang.

"Get back here!" Jet laughed into the radio. "Ya cheater!"

"You kids behave up there," came Jericho's voice on the radio. "I don't need a dressing down by Midnight if CHP tags us."

"I thought ya coppers got off with a warning," Quinn commented.

"Coppers?" Jericho responded. "What are we, old time gangsters?"

"Maybe just the old part," Jet put in.

"Watch it, missy," Lyric said this time.

"Sorry, Mama!" Jet put in, chuckling.

As the drive continued, Lyric could sense Savanna relaxing and she was glad. She knew this was something they needed. They really needed to reconnect; work had been hectic for both of them and between that and a toddler, they never seemed to have time for each other anymore. The last thing Lyric wanted was to lose her deep connection with her wife.

"So how are things at the house lately?" Lyric asked, referring to the LGBTQ home that Savanna ran.

"It's going okay," Savanna said. "We've been getting more and more kids though recently."

"Why do you think that is?"

Savanna shrugged. "Honestly, I'm not sure, but I think it has something to do with the attitude this administration seems to have about LGBTQ people in general. It seems like the country is starting to come apart at the seams a bit."

Savanna was referring to the policies of the Trump administration. There was a definite slant toward taking away LGBTQ rights. More and more issues were cropping up where protections for LGBTQ people were being threatened or downright taken away. There'd been a significant shift shortly after Trump had taken office; all information about LGBTQ rights and issues had been removed from the White House website. Transgender people had been barred from serving in the military, and many protections for transgender students had been removed. More recently he'd made it legal again to discriminate against members of the LGBTQ community in the workplace.

"And it's affecting the kids?" Lyric asked, sensing that Savanna needed to vent.

"It's trickling down to them." Savanna nodded. "When there's hate coming from the top office in the land, it seems to make people think they can suddenly say whatever they think. I've had more kids come in beaten and bruised in the last few months than I did for a year before that. It's getting worse and worse. This guy is making it okay to throw away kids that are gay. If their own president hates them… what are they supposed to think of themselves? I just hate this administration." Savanna scrubbed her face in frustration.

Lyric drew in a deep breath, blowing it out as she nodded. "I know what you mean. It's like so much hate is coming out right now, it's scary."

"Yeah, and it's coming down on my kids, and I don't like it," Savanna stated, her tone all mama-bear at that moment.

Lyric couldn't help but smile. She loved that Savanna considered every child that came through the doors of her center to be her kids. It was how Lyric had fallen in love with her in the first place, over Savanna's love and dedication to Cody. It had spoken volumes about Savanna's capacity to love and give of herself, and it was undeniably attractive to Lyric, even though she never thought of herself as a lesbian in those days.

"We'll get through this, babe," Lyric said, reaching over to hold Savanna's hand.

Savanna's sigh said a lot about how much she'd been carrying around in her heart lately. Lyric squeezed her wife's hand and made a mental note to pay closer attention to her burdens, and do her best to be there for her more.

"Are you sure this is how you want to be spending your time before your tour?" Quinn asked Xandy, not for the first time.

Xandy reached over to touch Quinn's leg. "I'm with you, that's all I want."

"I know, but…" Quinn began, feeling a bit guilty for pushing the matter.

"It will be good for me to unplug for ten days," Xandy told her. "I need to just relax and be."

"Very Zen-like, babe." Quinn grinned, winking at Xandy.

"I'm trying to adopt a better attitude about this whole stardom thing."

"I know." Quinn chuckled. "But must we get so new-agey about it?"

"Do you want your wife stressed out, or calm?"

"Um, calm?"

"Don't make me call your mother," Xandy threatened.

Quinn gasped. "Thas below the belt."

Xandy laughed, poking her wife in the ribs. "Then be nice!"

Quinn growled, but the effect was spoiled by her sidelong smile. "So where are we goin' on this tour?"

"You'd know if you were at the meeting with me…" Xandy said in a singsongy voice.

"Yeah, yeah." Quinn held a hand up in surrender. "I know, but I told you I had that gig lined up that day, so, give me the lowdown again."

Xandy gave her wife a sour look, knowing she should be happy that Quinn was going with her on the tour. Wynter wasn't that lucky—Remington had booked a job before the tour had been scheduled.

"Fine," Xandy finally said, "well, you know we start in Belfast, so we can see your family for a little bit that day."

Quinn nodded, happy about that. She'd already seen them not too long ago for the wedding, but that didn't mean she didn't love the idea of seeing them again.

"Then we're in Dublin, then Scotland, and we do the New Year's Eve show in London. Then we're pretty much everywhere in Europe. I can't even remember all the places!"

"It's gonna be a long, grueling one from what I heard," Quinn said grimly. Europe in fall and winter may seem exciting to the tourists, but it was going to be cold, and Quinn was not looking forward to it. She was, however, glad she'd be with her wife.

"So we sleep on the floor?" Fadiyah was asking Jet, still not sure she understood the purpose of camping.

"Well, some people do, yes, but I got us an inflatable mattress to keep us up off the ground. I'd be lucky if I could move after a night of sleeping on the ground," Jet said, rolling her shoulder with just the thought of sleeping on cold ground.

"And people do this… on purpose?" Fadiyah asked, looking skeptical.

Jet threw her head back laughing, realizing how ridiculous it probably sounded to someone that had grown up in a hut in the middle of a desert. She nodded, even as she wiped her eyes. "Yes, babe, we Americans are weird like that." Fadiyah widened her eyes and screwed up her lips in a grimace. "It'll be fun," Jet assured her wife.

"If you say then it is so," Fadiyah responded, still sounding a bit doubtful.

They were both silent for a bit. Then Jet glanced over to see that Fadiyah was lost in thought.

"What's up, babe?" Jet asked. "You're not still worried about sleeping in a tent, are you?"

"Hmm? Oh." Fadiyah laughed softly. "No, you said it will be fun, I will do my best to believe you. I was just thinking about starting work with Finley."

"Ohhh the new job!" Jet exclaimed. "Well, you worked your butt off to get your nursing degree, I'm glad you're going to get to use it now."

"I am very excited to work with Finley, I think I will learn even more."

"You probably will. Maybe you'll want to become a doctor someday."

Fadiyah's face lit up with the thought. "Do you really think I could?"

Jet reached over, taking Fadiyah's hand in hers and smiling. "I think you can do anything you want, babe, that's what's great about America. You just have to have the drive to go out and get what you want."

"But are those degrees not very expensive to get? Do you think someone like me could get student loans?" Fadiyah stumbled over the words since they were so unfamiliar to her. She'd heard many times in her nursing classes that doctors were in deep debt due to these "student loans."

"You wouldn't need student loans, babe. I'd pay if you wanted to do it."

Fadiyah shook her head. "I could not ask you to pay so much, Jet."

"Well, you wouldn't be asking, I'd be offering," Jet told her. "Fadi, I want you to do what you want with your life. Is being a doctor something you think you would want to do?"

Fadiyah looked serious for a long moment, but then shrugged in uncertainty. "I am not sure what I want."

"And that's okay too," Jet reassured her. "I'm just saying that if you did want to go in that direction, I'd be behind you all the way. Okay?"

Fadiyah inhaled deeply, even as she bit her lower lip, her eyes glazing with tears. "You are so good to me."

"I love you, that's what you do for people you love. You take care of them, and you support their dreams."

"Like your dream to sleep in a tent." Fadiyah smiled mischievously.

Jet threw her wife a vile look, but laughed as she did. "Now you're getting it," she said with a wink.

The group stopped for breakfast in Bakersfield, pulling into a Denny's restaurant. Everyone got out and stretched, and then headed inside. As they commandeered an entire corner of the restaurant, there was the usual level of mayhem.

"I need food!" Shenin said. "We got so busy this morning we forgot to even grab coffee."

"How do you survive without coffee?" Jet sounded horrified by the thought.

"Well, I'm sure they don't drink the jet fuel that you do," Quinn commented.

"You should talk," Xandy told her wife. "A spoon could stand up in your coffee with no help at all."

"It's good Irish coffee, thas why," Quinn retorted.

"The stuff I drink is from the Middle East, so it's pretty strong, but it's good. I already miss it…" Jet mused.

"I brought some with us," Fadiyah assured her wife.

"And that is why I love you…" Jet smiled, batting her eyelashes at Fadiyah.

"That better not be the only reason," Jericho put in.

"Nah, she's really cute too." Jet winked at Fadiyah.

Aiden fussed, and Shenin started to lean over to pick him up out of the car seat.

"Let me," Zoey said, smiling. "I haven't gotten to hold him since last week!"

Jericho and Quinn exchanged an amused look. "As much as I know you want to say it," Jericho told Quinn ominously, "don't say it."

"Say what?" Zoey asked as she bounced Aiden to calm him. Her look went between Jericho and Quinn suspiciously.

"Nothing." Quinn's face was the epitome of innocence, and Xandy elbowed her wife in the ribs.

"Behave," Xandy told the feisty Irishwoman.

"I—" Quinn began.

"Just behave." Xandy cut her off with pursed lips as she shook her head.

The rest of the table laughed at the conversation. It was rare that Xandy was bossy with Quinn, but everyone enjoyed it thoroughly when she was. For all of Quinn's bluster, Xandy could wrap her around her little finger and make her do anything she wanted. It was quite literally the cutest thing most of them had ever seen.

The waitress approached their tables, her eyes scanning the large group, her pen poised. She snapped her gum waiting for the group to notice her. She was hard to miss at a good six feet with bright pink hair all piled on top of her head in a wild beehive. Her uniform was tight and short, and she wore bright pink tennis shoes. Her name tag said "Flo" and they all got a vision of the character from the 1970s show *Alice* that frequently enjoined people to "kiss my grits!"

"How y'all this morning?" she asked, her southern drawl evident and went perfectly with the character they were thinking about.

"We're good, and you?" Jericho asked.

"I'm fair to midland," Flo informed them, smiling cheekily. The group chuckled, enjoying the colorful waitress. "So what are y'all drinkin'?"

The drink orders went in, with Jet asking if they had any espresso. She got a blank stare for the answer. "There's that foofy coffee place over yonder," Flo told Jet, gesturing toward Starbucks. "You could try there."

"Thanks." Jet nodded, doing her best not to sigh loudly.

After drinks were delivered, food was ordered and the group settled into a discussion of the next leg of their journey.

"So it's about three and a half hours from here to Yosemite," Lyric told them. "Obviously we can stop along the way if anyone needs to, but hopefully, we should get there"—she glanced at her watch—"right about one thirty or so."

"I got us booked at Pinecrest Campground, it's near a lake, so it should be nice," Savanna said. "We've got a space for the camper, and I booked three tent sites right next to us, so we should be close to each other."

Everyone nodded, happy that Savanna had thought of booking, since none of them had even thought to reserve a spot.

"Thanks for doing that," Shenin said to Savanna. "I've been so crazed at work since we had to relocate I haven't had time to think about much else."

"Me either," Jet agreed. "I was still in Washington, D.C. this time yesterday."

"Yikes!" Tyler, who'd often made that trip when she was stationed at Joint Andrews Air Base and Shenin was in California, knew what a grueling trek it could be.

"Tell me about it." Jet grimaced. "I just got home at three this morning!"

"Okay," Jericho spoke up, always the stern adult figure in the group. "So no more racing antics, I don't want anyone in an accident on this trip." She pinned Jet with a look. "You make sure you get some caffeine into you, and you let us know if you need to stop."

"Ma'am, yes, ma'am," came Jet's snappy reply, even as she smiled at the other woman, appreciating that she cared.

"Good thinking on the reservations, Savanna, thanks," Quinn put in.

"Definitely, excellent," Tyler said, smiling at Savanna, who accepted all the thank yous with a simple nod and smile. Savanna was used to having to organize things for lots of people so this was nothing new to her.

As food started to arrive, Shenin stood to take Aiden from Zoey, who hugged the now sleeping little boy closer. "I can hold him," Zoey told her, "you eat."

Shenin smiled. "Thanks, I'll eat fast."

"Take your time," Zoey said, looking like she was thoroughly enjoying holding the baby.

When they were back on the road, Jericho looked over at Zoey, who was still smiling. She'd held Aiden right up until they'd left the restaurant, insisting on carrying him to the car. It was obvious the girl was smitten.

"So," Jericho began carefully, "would you want one of our own?"

Zoey looked over at Jericho, her blue eyes wide. "You mean a baby?"

"No, I mean an espresso." Jericho grinned, since they'd all had to wait for Jet to get her fix before they could get on the road again.

"Fun-ny…" Zoey said, giving Jericho a narrowed look.

"Yes, I mean a baby, honey." Jericho laughed. Zoey bit her lip, her eyes saying everything she didn't. "So I'm guessing that's a yes."

"I just never thought…" Zoey began, spreading her hands plaintively. "I mean, you and Kelly never…"

Jericho grimaced. "It was hard enough having a dog with her, babe, and you see how that turned out."

"I know, but I just didn't know if you two were ever planning it, and… well, you know, maybe you never wanted kids."

Jericho looked thoughtful for a long moment. "The fact of the matter is, I never really thought that much about it. I mean, it was out of the question with Kelly, because she was far too selfish with her time, attention, and heart to share it with a child. So, I guess I'd figured I wasn't ever going to have kids."

"But you're thinking about it now?" Zoey's tone held so much hope that it was almost painful. In response, Jericho took Zoey's hand and lifted it to her lips.

"With you, yes, I'm thinking about it."

"We're not even married yet, though," Zoey pointed out.

"About that…" Jericho said, smiling. "You know, we were originally waiting for you to get your doctorate. That happened a year ago and still no plans for a wedding… Why is that?"

Zoey looked back at Jericho with an openmouthed stare, then she closed her mouth slowly, shaking her head. "I honestly have no idea."

Jericho chuckled. "Well, that's an honest answer. Maybe all this career hunting has kept you off track?"

"Probably."

After Zoey had received her doctorate, she'd set about looking for a job to utilize that degree. Many of the options she'd been offered weren't things she felt her degree would be useful for. Recently, however, the newly elected Governor for the State of California, Midnight Chevalier, had seen fit to contact Zoey personally and offer her a job on her staff.

Her position was called a Career Executive Assignment, which meant that Midnight was able to appoint her to head her California for All Women program. It was an exciting opportunity for Zoey, and she'd been beyond honored that Midnight had chosen her. She was set to start her new job in the beginning of the year.

"So now that that's settled, should we just go ahead and do it?" Jericho asked. Her tone was so conversational that it took Zoey a minute to understand what she was saying.

"You mean… get married?" Zoey stammered.

Jericho quirked her lips in a grin. "Yeah, get married."

"Uh, when?" Zoey asked haltingly.

Jericho shrugged. "Maybe there's somewhere in Yosemite to get married."

"So you mean, on this trip?" It was clear from the look on Zoey's face she thought Jericho was losing her mind.

Jericho laughed. "I'm just saying we could."

"On this trip," Zoey repeated.

"I'm guessing that's a negatory on the campsite nuptials," Jericho surmised.

"I'm not getting married to the love of my life in jeans and hiking boots!" Zoey stated emphatically.

"Okay, okay, it was just a thought, sheesh," Jericho replied, her dark eyes sparkling with humor.

Zoey blew out her breath, giving her fiancée a vile look. "You just amaze me sometimes."

"Happy to help." Jericho winked at Zoey and received a smack on the arm for it.

"But, yes, I would love to have a child with you, Jericho Tehrani."

"Well, then that'll be the plan, Zoey Cabbott."

By one o'clock that afternoon they were heading for the campground. They pulled into the wooded area, with huge redwood trees all around them. After finding their spots, everyone started setting up their camp.

"Jerich, can you just come help me?" Quinn enquired after trying to work with Xandy for over half an hour. "I'll help you when we're done." The last was said as she cast an eye at Jericho and Zoey's half-assed attempt to set up a tent.

"Deal!" Jericho agreed readily, ignoring Zoey's grunt of annoyance.

Neither Zoey nor Xandy had ever been camping, and therefore were very unfamiliar with how to put up a tent. The two younger women looked at each other and shrugged.

"I saw a store when we drove in, want to walk over there and see what they have?" Zoey asked Xandy.

"Sounds like a great plan!" Xandy responded enthusiastically.

The two grabbed their purses and walked over to where Shenin and Fadiyah stood watching Jet and Tyler wrestle with Jet's tent.

"We're going to the store," Zoey told Shenin and Fadiyah, "wanna come?"

"Absolutely," Shenin answered immediately.

"Oh, yes please." Fadiyah sounded very relieved.

As Jet and Tyler watched the women walk away they grinned at each other.

"I figured they'd get bored soon," Tyler joked.

"I don't think Fadiyah wanted to hear one more cuss word," Jet replied. "Hopefully they'll buy some beer."

"Let's get this damned thing up while they're gone!"

"Can I hold him?" Zoey gestured to Aiden who sat in his cozy hanging in front of Shenin.

"Sure!" Shenin happily agreed. "He's starting to give me a backache!"

"I need to start getting some practice." Zoey grinned slyly.

"Are you and Jericho thinking of doing this!" Xandy asked, looking excited.

"Yep!" Zoey replied happily.

"That's fantastic!" Shenin enthused.

"Quinn and I are going to talk about it, but Quinn thinks BJ will be mad," Xandy told them.

"It's your life, Xandy," Zoey told her, holding Aiden and making faces at him. "He doesn't own you."

"I know." Xandy sighed. "But I really hate it when he gets mad at me."

When they finally got to the store, they found it to be decently stocked with various items. There were a number of souvenirs too, so the girls had a great time buying T-shirts, sweatshirts, sweatpants, scarves, and whatever else struck their fancy. Shenin bought a couple of cases of beer, and some extra bags of chips and sodas.

"Should we get another case of water?" Shenin asked the group.

"Water's always a good thing," Xandy said.

"Definitely!" Zoey agreed.

Fadiyah nodded as she pulled on a warm winter hoodie. She'd been cold since they'd gotten to the park.

"Sheesh, maybe we should have brought one of the cars," Shenin said, as the cashier rang up their numerous purchases.

"Oh my God, you're Xandy Blue, aren't you!" one of the other cashiers, a young man, gushed.

Xandy smiled and nodded.

"Can you sign this for me?" The young man handed Xandy his hat, his eyes sparkling with delight. "And you know if you ladies need help bringing this to your car or whatever I can help you!"

"Well, there you go," Shenin murmured to Zoey.

Back at the campsite, Lyric and Savanna were having problems. The leveling of the camper had become an issue; Lyric thought she had to put a board down to level it out, but it turned out the leveling jacks were electric, and it was just a matter of figuring out which button did what. Then getting the "plumbing" grey water tank hooked up, so they could actually utilize the sinks, toilet and shower, wasn't easy either. The owner of the camper, Frank, had given Lyric a quick rundown, but Lyric hadn't mentally captured everything he'd said. It was one thing to hear about something, quite another to actually have to handle it when you got to the site.

"I need to do what?" Savanna asked from inside the camper.

"I need you to Google 'black water tank' versus 'grey water tank'!"

"Wow, okay, that's a new one," Savanna muttered to herself as she pulled out her phone. After reading for a moment, and grimacing, she called back, "Black water is the icky stuff, you know poop and stuff. Grey water is the stuff from the sink and shower. It's two different tanks."

"And I care about that because?" Lyric called back.

"Well, I guess you are hooking up the hose thingy to the drain spout that does both the black and grey water."

"And that hooks up under here."

"Babe, I can't see where 'here' is!"

"Ouch! Goddamn it!" Lyric yelled. "Oh, this shit stinks…"

"Well, it's shit so…" Savanna muttered to herself, knowing Lyric couldn't hear her.

"This fucking thing won't go on!" Lyric yelled.

"What can I do?" Savanna called back.

"Shoot me?"

"I'm thinking the department would frown upon that."

"Probably!" Lyric said, as she kept messing with the hose, attempting to attach it to the drain spout to empty the water tanks. "Remind me to use some gloves next time, I'm going to need a shower by the time I'm done out here!"

Savanna grinned, then answered a text from Cody about whether Ana could have tomatoes or not.

"Finally!" Lyric yelled in triumph. "Now, I need you to turn on the water, to see if it's working!" Lyric called.

"Oh… kay," Savanna said, having noted the irritation in Lyric's voice. It was obvious her wife was out of her element and hating it. She turned on the faucet, which sputtered a bit, then the water began running. "Yep! It works!"

"Great!" Lyric called back. "Now I'm going to try to plug in the electricity thingy. Let me know if any of the lights come on!"

"Okey dokey!" Savanna called back. She sat and waited inside, admiring the nice camper. The agent at the department who owned it had kept it in great condition. The camper itself was only two years old. It was thirty-two feet long and had a "master bedroom," a dining area, kitchen and living area, a nice sized bathroom with a shower, and even a separate room with a door with bunk beds and a small table. It was a very nice set up.

The lights flicked on. "Got it!" Savanna yelled.

A couple of minutes later, Lyric walked into the camper. Her shirt was a mess, and she was holding her hands out away from her sides.

"I feel gross," Lyric said.

Savanna made a face and immediately walked toward the bathroom, reaching in to turn on the shower. Then she gestured to her wife.

"Take all of that off and get into the shower." Lyric did as she was told, but the water was freezing. "Damnit, I think we need to light the pilot light for the water heater."

"Well, this camping thing is harder than it looks," Savanna observed, as she held Lyric's robe. "At least wash your hands thoroughly before I hand you this."

Lyric rolled her eyes, but did as she was told, washing all the way up to her elbows with soap and water. Once she'd dried her hands and arms she put her warm bathrobe on and went to look at the panel for lighting the pilot light.

"Well, that'll take forever," Lyric said, heading to the bedroom to pull out some clothes to put on. It was already starting to get dark outside and she wanted to get a fire started.

Xandy arrived back at the campsite with a golf cart and all of their purchases, and Chet the cashier driving.

"What all did you buy?" Quinn asked as Chet busily started unloading the cart. "And where is everyone else?"

"Oh, they're coming," Xandy said, laughing. "We couldn't fit all of this and all of us at the same time."

"Uh-huh…" Quinn murmured, as she watched Chet unload. "And who's your friend?"

"Oh, Quinn this is Chet, Chet, this is my wife, Quinn." Xandy smiled.

It was obvious Quinn was on alert, never trusting men who helped her pop star wife, figuring there was always an angle. To her surprise Chet smiled wider and extend his hand to Quinn happily.

"You're the White Knight!" Chet exclaimed excitedly. "It's an honor to meet you!"

Xandy immediately hid her laugh behind her hand, even as Quinn narrowed her eyes at her wife. To Chet, however, Quinn was very kind, and thanked him for helping Xandy and the girls with their purchases.

"Three cases of water, babe? Seriously?" Tyler asked as they stacked the water near the camper.

"Well, there's ten of us, I figured we should stay hydrated!"

"That shouldn't be a problem," Lyric observed, as she unloaded firewood from the camper's storage.

"Oh, they have firewood too, if we need more before we leave." Shenin smiled, giving Lyric a wink.

"Good to know," Lyric replied.

Later, they set about making dinner, with the bois handling the "grilling" over the fire ring, and the women handling the side dishes and dessert.

The meal was accomplished without too many complications, except for a discussion about the best way to grill a burger.

After dinner, they all sat around the campfire, talking about random subjects and just enjoying the night sounds.

"So what do we want to do tomorrow?" Lyric asked.

"I want to try out the Four Mile Trail," Jet said, lifting a beer to her lips.

"I take it it's actually four miles?" Shenin asked.

"That's what they say." Jet nodded. "What I read said it's a moderate to strenuous trail, but the views are supposed to be spectacular."

"I'm in," Tyler said, clinking her bottle with Jet's.

"Yeah, I'd like to give that a shot too," Quinn agreed.

"Count me in too," Jericho said.

"I guess I'll give it a shot." Lyric sighed. "I'm not sure I can keep up with you kids though."

"You can stay in the back with me." Jericho winked.

"That works." Lyric chuckled.

"So what do you girls want to do?" Savanna asked the rest.

"I want to go to Mirror Lake, the reflections are supposed to be beautiful." Shenin smiled, having heard of the lake a few times over the years.

"Oh that sounds nice," Zoey said. "I'm all in on that one."

"Me too," Xandy agreed.

"I will go too," Fadiyah said.

"Well, then I guess that's decided," Savanna proclaimed. "Do you want us to pack you bois some food for the trail?"

"You'd be my new favorite person," Jet told Savanna.

"I'm not your favorite person now?" Savanna queried with a raised eyebrow.

Jet dropped her head in mock chagrin. "Of course you are."

"Yadda, yadda, yadda," Quinn teased. "Savanna it would be excellent of you if you would make us some sandwiches or something to take with us."

"There you go, bein' all smooth again…" Jericho commented.

"Thas just who I am, lass." Quinn winked comically at Jericho.

"I got your lass," Jericho warned with a crooked grin.

"Bois, bois, you're both pretty," Tyler put in with a laugh, and was rewarded by having marshmallows lobbed at her.

As it got late, everyone retired to their tents. Shenin and Tyler who were bunking with Lyric and Savanna, went into their "room" in the camper. Aiden was happily ensconced in his travel bassinet on one of the bunk beds. Shenin had put sheets on the pull-out bed on the other side of the back room.

"It's getting frigging cold out there!" Tyler said as she entered the room, having helped ensure that the campfire was properly put out.

"Yeah, temps drop when the sun goes down out here," Shenin said.

"No lie about that!"

"Do you think Aiden will be warm enough?" Shenin worried.

"Babe, you've got him in a blanket sleeper, and he's tucked in with another blanket. I think he'll be fine."

"Okay, I'm just worried…"

"I know, babe." Tyler took Shenin in her arms, hugging her, and kissing the top of her head. "Man, I'm beat!"

"Yeah, I guess we should never underestimate all this fresh air, huh?" Shenin chuckled, thinking that Tyler really had done a lot of physical work that day with helping unload and set up camp. The girls had been gone shopping long enough to avoid most of that work.

"Nope," Tyler agreed, "and I want to be ready for this hike tomorrow."

"I'm glad you brought those hiking boots! We don't need any turned ankles or anything."

"Don't say that!" Tyler exclaimed. "You'll jinx us!"

Shenin grimaced. "Oops, sorry."

"Sheesh, you've been out too long." Tyler winked.

"Shaddup!" Shenin pushed at Tyler's shoulder, giving her a narrowed look. "Remember you're retired now too!"

"Don't remind me!" Tyler cried.

"Don't wake up the baby!" Shenin whispered, covering Tyler's mouth with her hand.

"Then don't say mean things to me," Tyler mumbled behind Shenin's hand.

"This is nice," Savanna said, as she and Lyric lay in the comfortable king-sized bed. "Do you like it?"

Lyric, who lay on her side facing her wife, slid her hand over Savannah's waist, pulling her closer as she nuzzled her neck. "It's very nice."

"I meant the camper, silly," Savanna chided.

"The camper is nice too," Lyric agreed. "Lots of room, nice amenities like heating and all that. Frank definitely kept it in nice condition."

"And how much is he asking for the whole thing? He's selling the truck too, right?"

"Yeah, he wants like sixty thousand for all of it," Lyric said, hoping Savanna wasn't going to have a coronary at that figure.

Predictably, Savanna's lips twitched; she was usually the more careful one about money. "How much did you say a camper like this would cost if we bought one?"

"From what I looked up, about forty to forty-five thousand."

"And the truck?"

"About another forty."

"Wow, so it is a good price…" Savanna murmured.

"Yeah, it is." Lyric's tone was leading. She had already decided she really liked the camper and the truck, but she wasn't sure what Savanna would say.

"How are we going to afford it?" Savanna queried, knowing that Lyric would already have a plan in mind. Lyric did indeed.

"I'm thinking we sell the Ducati."

Savanna was shocked. "You love that bike."

"I do." Lyric nodded. "But we rarely ride anymore, and last time I took too long of a ride every body part I own got stiff. So maybe it's time for a change."

"And you think you can get sixty thousand for it?"

"I think I can get close, if not all of it."

"Cody will be bummed, she loves that bike," Savanna pointed out.

"Well, I could offer it to her."

"They can't afford that, babe," Savanna said. "And no, you're not giving them a 'deal' on it. I really don't want Cody riding that bike, it's too fast. If you want to sell her something, sell her the Indian."

Lyric had traded Jet a custom Harley Davidson motorcycle to buy the Ducati Superleggera from her three years before. It had been worth it since Jet had only asked forty-five thousand for a sixty-five-thousand-dollar bike. Now one motorcycle could buy them a camper and a truck. To Lyric it was worth the deal. She still had a custom Indian Roadmaster in her garage, so it wasn't like she wouldn't have a motorcycle anymore.

"We'd have to find a good way to store the camper," Lyric indicated. "Maybe we could get Dakota to fix us up a gate on the west side of the house, and we could pour a cement pad back there."

"So you have been planning this, huh?" Savanna accused.

"Well, no, I just considered what ifs, in case we liked it." Lyric held up her hands in surrender.

"Mmmhmm…" Savanna murmured. "Sure."

Lyric's smile was far from innocent. To distract her suspicious wife she leaned in nuzzling Savanna's neck, kissing it softly and then moving to her ear.

"But you still love me, right?" Lyric's voice was husky and sexy and it gave Savanna a shiver of sheer delight.

"I hate that I'm so easy when it comes to you." Savanna did her best to sound annoyed, and failed.

"Yes, but you love why you're so easy with me," Lyric informed her, her lips moving to Savanna's lips.

Savanna moaned softly. "Jesus, do you think this camper is soundproof?"

Lyric chuckled softly. "Probably not."

"Then behave!" Savanna whispered urgently.

That had Lyric laughing.

"Get closer!" Xandy told Quinn as she shivered again. "It's so damned cold!"

"I'm as close as I can get, love," Quinn informed her wife.

"Well, it's not close enough, I swear I'm freezing!"

"You've lived in California too long, love, it's thinned your blood."

"Well, you promised to love, honor and keep me warm not too long ago, so get to it!" Xandy scolded.

Quinn pulled Xandy impossibly closer from behind, wrapping her arms tighter around the smaller woman. "I really don't remember there being a part about keeping you warm in the vows, love."

"Don't sass me!" Xandy told her wife.

Quinn's chest rumbled in a low chuckle. "Yes, dear."

"Did you know that Jericho and Zoey are talking about kids?"

Quinn blinked a couple of times, surprised by the sudden change in conversation. "No, I didn't know that."

"I was surprised too, but I guess it makes sense."

"Makes sense?" Quinn queried, trying to catch up.

"Well, Jericho is what, like forty-two now?"

Quinn nodded, her look circumspect.

Xandy sensed it, glancing over her shoulder at Quinn. "What?"

"Nothing."

"You're worried that I'm going to say you're forty now and think we should have kids too, right?" Xandy predicted correctly.

"Maybe," Quinn responded with a smirk.

"I know you're almost the same age as Jericho, but she's just so much more…" Xandy's voice trailed off and Quinn's eyebrow lifted.

"Are you about to say more mature?" Quinn accused.

"No!" Xandy huffed. "I was going to say older."

Quinn pursed her lips, thinking that her dear, sweet wife was telling a half truth. The fact was, Quinn Kavanaugh had always been much more serious, before she'd met and fallen in love with Xandy. Xandy had brought out Quinn's joy for life, and they'd built a life with friends around them that she enjoyed teasing. Quinn knew that her life was so much better for having love and friends in it, and she knew it had everything to do with Xandy.

"Well, Jericho has always been more mature than anyone I know, so, I guess it makes sense that she'd seem 'older' to you."

Xandy nodded, glad that she hadn't just insulted her wife. She loved Quinn more than anything in the whole world, and the last thing she wanted was to hurt her feelings. Quinn was fun loving, and often acted younger than her years because she had people around her who did the same. In truth, Xandy loved that Quinn had embraced her social side; their lives were full of people who loved them, and that they loved. For too many years, Xandy had kept to herself, even when she'd come to Los Angles for her music career, because she never knew who was genuine. Quinn Kavanaugh was the most genuine person she'd ever met. It was one of the many reasons she loved her.

"So were you wantin' a wee one then?" Quinn asked, sounding very Irish at that moment.

Xandy smiled at the phrase. "Yes, I'd love a wee one at some point."

"But not now?" Quinn clarified.

"I want to time it right, you know?"

"You mean you don't want to piss BJ off."

"I mean, I want to be between albums and tours and all this craziness."

Quinn nodded wisely, sure that her wife was worried about BJ. As the owner of the label Xandy was signed to, BJ had a lot of pull with his young star, but Quinn would be damned if BJ Sparks would ever stand in the way of Xandy's happiness.

"So what about after this tour?" Quinn asked bluntly.

"You mean when we get back?"

"Yeah."

"But we need to find a house."

"We have a house, babe."

"But we were going to look for something bigger, with a yard," Xandy worried.

"And so we shall. You don't have to be exactly where you want to be house-wise in order to have a baby, you know."

Xandy laughed softly. "I know that, but I thought that was what you wanted."

"I do want that," Quinn said, "but a wee one won't need a yard right away."

Xandy shifted, turning over to face Quinn. "So you're serious about doing this after the tour?"

"I am."

"Wow," Xandy commented. "You talked to the boys about donating, right?"

"Yes," Quinn confirmed. Much like others in their group, they'd asked for one of Quinn's brothers to donate sperm so the baby would look like Quinn too. Fortunately, Quinn had several brothers to choose from. "Miles is more than happy to donate. He said, he'd come stay here for a few months to be available. He wants to do some work with Scripps Institute down in San Diego, so it works for him."

"You had that good of a conversation, did you?" Xandy asked, very surprised.

"The bois got me thinking about it at the wedding, so I've been in touch with him to talk about it."

"So I owe the bois, huh?" Xandy smiled.

"You do."

"I'll hug the stuffing out of Jericho tomorrow."

"Good show." Quinn winked at Xandy. "Now, let's try to get some kip so I can make that hike tomorrow!"

"Is it supposed to be this cold?" Fadiyah asked Jet, as she did her best to snuggle down into the sleeping bag.

"Well, it is coming on toward winter, so yes it can be."

"It never gets this cold in Iraq," Fadiyah commented.

Jet grinned. "Well, no, babe, it's a desert, so no it doesn't."

Fadiyah gave her a foul look. "You did not warn me of this."

"I'm sorry!" Jet laughed. "I really didn't think about it."

"I feel like I'm going to be a cube-sicle in the morning!" Fadiyah said between chattering teeth.

"A popsicle?" Jet asked.

"Yes, one of those!"

"Why don't you put the sweatshirt on that you bought at the store?"

"A good idea!" Fadiyah agreed. "But then I would have to freeze even more to get out of the sleeping bag and put it on."

"Be fast?" Jet offered.

"Be quiet," Fadiyah said with a narrowed look, as she quickly got up and grabbed the sweatshirt, putting it on over her pajama top.

"Grab extra socks too, and pull the hood up over your head."

"Yes, I know, you lose heat from your head and your feet." Fadiyah nodded, reaching for her bag with her socks in it, even as she pulled her hood up too.

When Fadiyah was back inside the sleeping bag, Jet gave her a conciliatory look. "I'm really sorry, babe. I really didn't think to check the weather before we came."

"Tomorrow I am going back to that store and buying everything that is warm!"

"Good plan," Jet agreed, feeling bad for her wife, but also amused by her angry comments, as if the weather was doing this on purpose.

Chapter 3

The second day of their trip dawned bright and sunny. Regardless, there were lots of moans and groans elicited as each couple made their way out to the campfire. Lyric, who'd been first up that morning, had not only started a nice fire, but had two pots of coffee on the grill laid across the fire pit. She began handing out steaming cups as her friends arrived at the fire.

"I'm guessing it was cold out here last night," Lyric commented, as she surveyed the various layers of clothing worn by each of her friends.

"I nearly froze my arse off!" Quinn exclaimed grouchily.

"Yeah, I think we underestimated how cold it was going to be here…" Jet said, receiving a look full of vitriol from her wife.

"I miss the desert." Fadiyah sighed, making everyone chuckle.

"I'm guessing that camper was nice and warm." Jericho gestured to Shenin and Tyler emerging from inside.

"It was fantastic!" Shenin enthused, then grimaced seeing the angry looks she received. "It's definitely cold out here. Brrr!"

"Save it," Jet growled.

"I thought tent camping was the only way to go," Tyler commented, reminding Jet of her words the night of Thanksgiving.

"Bite me, Hancock!" Jet exclaimed, even as she shook her head with a smile. "It is the only way to go if it's not the damned artic north outside."

Everyone got a chuckle out of that.

"Hey, did that magic store you ladies went to happen to have personal heaters?" Lyric asked.

"I don't remember seeing any," Shenin replied. "But I wasn't really looking either. Did any of you notice any?"

Zoey, Fadiyah, and Xandy shook their heads.

"Damn," Quinn said, "maybe we can scout the local area to see if there are any stores that have some?"

"I think there are a few extension cords in the camper that we can use to run some power to the tents, to power heaters if we find them," Lyric told the group.

Jet immediately pulled out her phone to Google the area. "Not getting a signal in here. Anyone else?"

The others checked their phones, all shaking their heads.

"Maybe we can ask someone at the store if they know of anywhere around here," Jericho offered.

"Definitely a good idea." Shenin nodded.

After breakfast the bois got ready for their hike, while Xandy and Shenin, sporting Aiden in his snuggly around her shoulders, walked back over to the store at the campsite.

"Fadi, honey," Jet said, poking her head out of the camper after her fast shower, "where did you put my hair gel?"

Fadiyah immediately pressed her lips together in a grimace, her eyes wide.

"You didn't pack any," Jet surmised.

"I am so sorry, Jet."

Jet sighed, glancing at her friends watching this tableau. "Anyone got a hat?"

A chuckle ran through the group. No one was used to Jet without her signature spiked hair, so this would be new.

Five minutes later she sported a camouflage hat with the Hard Rock Café logo on the front, donated by Quinn.

Shenin and Xandy were able to talk to a couple of the employees and came back with good news and bad news.

"So I have good news and bad news. The good news is if we go over to Highway 108, right out here"—Shenin pointed to the road off to the west of the campsite—"head south, and in about eighteen miles we'll hit Twain Harte Lumber and Ace Hardware. They said if we're going to find any heaters this time of year, it's going to be there."

"Great! Well, we can maybe go after our hike." Jericho nodded.

"Uh, well." Shenin grimaced. "The bad news is that apparently we're dorks and don't realize how big Yosemite is." She gave Fadiyah and Zoey an apologetic look. "Apparently Mirror Lake is about a hundred miles away from here, if we drive."

"Oh, bad luck there, love," Quinn said.

"Not so fast, babe," Xandy said, grinning. "Apparently the Four Mile Trail is just as far away. We really didn't stay in a good part of the park for this stuff."

"Damn it!" Savanna lamented. "I should have checked that out. I'm sorry, guys."

"Hey, you're the only one that thought to make a reservation here, babe, it's okay." Lyric hugged Savanna.

"I know, but…" Savanna buried her head in Lyric's shoulder, feeling really bad for not knowing any better.

"Lyric's right, Savanna," Jet agreed, "we all could have done more research. We'll find something else to do around here, don't worry."

"I grabbed a map thinking the same thing!" Shenin smiled as she pulled the map out of her pocket.

"That's my girl!" Tyler said, poking a finger in the air to indicate she'd just won.

They laid the map out on the picnic table in their campsite and started looking at what was in the area.

"Looks like Yosemite Village isn't a bad drive, maybe an hour or two," Jet observed.

"Yeah, we'd go right by that Twain Harte area, so we could hit up the hardware store on the way by."

Jericho checked her watch. "It's only 8:30, we could get down there by ten or so, and still have time to maybe get in some hiking."

"Then let's go!" Quinn exhorted.

"Savanna, you and Lyric can ride with us," Jericho told the couple.

"Great, thanks!" Lyric said. "Let's get some snacks and stuff together for the hike, but we can be ready to go in about twenty minutes."

Twenty-five minutes later, the group piled into the cars and got on the road. In Twain Harte they had some success finding personal heaters, picking up two, which was all they had left.

"You and Fadi can bunk with us," Jericho offered. "Our tent is made for six, so two more shouldn't crowd us too much."

"Sounds good." Jet nodded.

Another hour and half later, they made it down to Yosemite Village. They made the drive that toured the most famous sites that Yosemite boasted, such as the sheer cliff face that was El Capitan, and views of Half Dome. After checking out the sights from the road, they decided to stop and have an early lunch. They ended up at The Base Camp Eatery, which offered a few different options for lunch in a cafeteria style atmosphere. It was a bit crowded, but they finally found a place to eat together.

"It's turned out to be a nice day," Lyric commented, noting the blue skies and sunshine.

"Yeah, and it looks like our hike is just up the road a bit," Quinn said, having finally gotten a signal on her phone to look it up.

"Awesome!" Jet exalted. "Maybe you girls can still make Mirror Lake today too."

Shenin was already busy on her phone. "Yep! It's just twenty minutes from here. Cool!"

"Yay!" Xandy cheered. "See, Savanna? It turns out we freaked out for nothing."

Savanna looked relieved, appreciating that everyone was trying to make her feel better.

After lunch, everyone headed in their separate directions. The girls made their way to the parking area where the hike into Mirror Lake started. It was a short hike, but still long enough to have most of them panting by the time they reached the area known as Mirror Lake.

"Well, I don't understand this…" Shenin said as she looked out over the dry, sandy area.

Mirror Lake was known for the beautiful, still water that reflected the surrounding mountains. The area they were standing in front of had no water whatsoever.

"Isn't there supposed to be a lake here?" Zoey asked someone standing nearby.

"There's only water in Mirror Lake during the late Spring or early Summer," the young man said.

Shenin sighed mightily. "Well, this sucks."

"We're just having the worst luck today," Xandy said, shaking her head.

"It is still beautiful here." Fadiyah beamed, her eyes shining. "The mountains are magnificent against the blue sky. And look!" Her voice dropped to a whisper. "There's a deer over there." Fadiyah pointed, and everyone around them turned to look.

Sure enough, there was a deer grazing in the meadow at the edge of the sandy depression that would have been the lake. She lifted her head, as if sensing that many eyes were suddenly on her. The deer chewed disinterestedly.

"There's a fawn!" Xandy whispered urgently.

You could feel the excitement in the group gathered on the side of the lake bed as the much smaller deer, still sporting spots, walked into the clearing and over to its mother.

"So beautiful…" Zoey breathed.

"I just want to cuddle the little guy." Savanna sighed.

"Me too," Fadiyah said breathlessly. She was truly amazed by the beauty of the moment she was witnessing.

Shenin had the presence of mind to pull out her phone to take pictures of the doe and fawn.

Meanwhile, the bois were trekking along on the Four Mile Trail. They'd made it to the view of Sentinel Rock, a tombstone-shaped rock that towered over the Yosemite Valley.

"Wow, now that's a view," Jericho said as they stood trying to catch their breath and look out at the panoramic view.

"Getting it all on camera," Jet told them, pointing to the Go Pro she'd affixed to her tactical vest.

"Nice!" Quinn clapped Jet on the shoulder.

"Not so much if one of us dies of exhaustion on this little trek," Lyric put in, as she sat on a rock, doing her best to catch her breath.

"This is great! What are you talking about?" Tyler asked, not even breaking a sweat at that point.

"Shaddup you!" Lyric growled. "Not all of us just retired from being a damned MP for the Air Force, okay?"

"Easy there, don't want you to have a heart attack or anything," Tyler said, winking at Lyric to show she was kidding.

Lyric shook her head, reaching up to wipe her brow. "I'm just a bit fatigued today for some reason, maybe I didn't sleep as good as I thought last night because of sleeping in a strange place."

The others nodded. Lyric got up off the rock and gestured toward the trail. "Let's get on with it."

The group trekked on. By the time they reached the end of the trail they were all sweating, even Tyler.

"Ugh!" Lyric moaned as she pulled off her sweatshirt and tied it around her waist. "I feel hot and disgusting."

"Here, drink some more water, that will help cool you down," Tyler told her, handing her a bottle of water from her pack. "We better hump it back though," she said, looking out over the valley. "It's gonna get dark fast and then it's gonna get cold."

"Yeah, I really don't want to be on this mountain and some of those super narrow parts of the trail in the dark, thank you very much," Jet said.

"Agreed!" Quinn put in.

"Let's take another five minutes, then head out," Jericho said.

They all stared out over the valley, enjoying the view. The panoramic picture of the valley below them was beyond incredible. With massive rocks rising out of the valley, glistening in the sun, and dazzling with the incredible size. It was easy to be humbled before the nature that lay before them. Mother Nature had done some seriously beautiful work in Yosemite Valley.

"Alright, let's head out," Tyler said, sounding like a military drill sergeant. That only got worse as they headed back down the trail. The sun was setting quickly, and they realized that they'd underestimated how long it would take. "Let's go, let's go!" Tyler ordered, worried about the impending darkness once the sun went down. It was already getting really cold. "Watch your footing here," she told her friends as they skirted large rocks. She did not want anyone getting hurt on this trip.

They were just about down when Jet slipped on some loose rocks and slid down the steep dirt and gravel hill for a good ten feet, yelling as the rocks ripped at exposed skin. The other bois ran down after her. Jericho, with her long strides, managed to get in ahead of Jet to help stop her descent.

"I got you!" Jericho told Jet, squatting down to ensure that Jet would slide no further.

"Jesus, fuck!" Jet yelled, feeling scraped in a number of places. "That could have been bad," she said, glancing around Jericho. Another five feet and she would have careened right over the edge of the cliff face. It was a long drop on that part of the trail.

The other four looked in the same direction and realized how close they'd come to losing their friend.

"So maybe a little less hustle," Tyler quipped, getting a laugh from the group, fortunately breaking the terrifying tension that had hit them when they'd seen how close Jet had come. At that point they hadn't had a cell phone signal for a long time; calling help would mean getting all the way down the mountain and that would mean either carrying Jet or leaving her up there in the dark. Neither option sounded good.

"Can you get up?" Jericho asked, even as Quinn moved to Jet's side to help her.

"Yeah…" Jet said, wincing as she did. "I feel like I'm bleeding all over."

"Do you feel like anything is broken?" Tyler asked, realizing that they were screwed if Jet needed any real medical attention. They weren't likely to get any very quickly at this time of day.

Jet tested putting her weight on the ankle that had taken the brunt of the slide. She nodded. "Yeah, I think I'm okay."

"Good, thank the gods," Quinn said, blowing out her breath. "It's getting darker, guys, let's go. Jet, do you need help?"

"I'm alright," Jet said, gritting her teeth. In truth her ankle hurt quite a bit, but she knew that there was no help for it right now. She did not want to be on that mountain trail in the dark, so they needed to get going now.

The group moved quickly but carefully down the rest of the trail. By the time they got to the bottom, however, Jet's ankle was swollen to twice its size.

"Okay, you stay here with her," Jericho told Quinn. "We'll go grab the car and bring it over."

"Got it." Quinn nodded, helping Jet sit down on a large rock nearby.

Jericho, Tyler, and Lyric went off to get Jericho's car. Tyler called Shenin to find out where they were.

"Thank God!" Shenin exclaimed. "Where have you been! I've been worried sick!"

"Sorry, babe, that trail took a lot longer than we thought, but we're getting in the car now. Where are you?"

"We're back at camp, we were just discussing sending out the National Guard to find you."

Tyler grimaced; she knew Shenin was joking about the National Guard, but she also knew that Shenin was serious about being worried. "I'm sorry, I really am. Look, Jet slipped and shredded her leg and we think she might have sprained her ankle. Can you make sure there's some ice there for when we get back? Maybe go back to your favorite store?"

"Of course!" Shenin said. "We'll get dinner going too, I'm sure you bois are famished."

"Damned skippy!" Tyler agreed. She grew serious again for a moment. "I really am sorry I worried you, babe."

"As long as you're okay, that's what matters to me."

"I love you, we'll be there soon," Tyler said as she got into the back seat of the Hellcat.

"I love you, we'll be ready with beers and ice."

"You are my queen," Tyler told her. Shenin laughed before hanging up.

"They were worried?" Lyric asked, knowing that Savanna would be ready to chew nails by now.

"Yeah," Tyler reported, still feeling bad she'd worried Shenin. "But they know we're okay now, and they'll get things ready for when Jet gets there."

"Good thing we brought along a nurse," Jericho said, grinning.

It took a full two and a half hours, but they finally got back to the campsite. The pitch-black roads hadn't made traveling any easier.

"Glad I'm not hauling a camper in this," Lyric commented at one point.

The darkness was so complete, with no lights at all on the highway, it was a bit scary at times.

"Note to self, travel before dark!" Jericho said.

"And don't slip on a mountain," Jet put in.

"That too," Quinn said, rolling her eyes.

The minute the Hellcat drove into the campsite, the women there were mobilized. Shenin and Fadiyah helped get Jet out of the passenger seat, sitting her in a chair with her ankle up on box so Fadiyah could take a good look at it. They'd brought out two camping lanterns to give her plenty of light to work with.

"Good thing we brought you extra pants," Fadiyah said as she took out her scissors to cut away the tattered jeans so she could get to her wounds.

"Damn…" Jet said, as her leg was exposed.

"Ouch." Zoey grimaced.

"Trust me, this is much better than it could have been," Quinn said, garnering a quelling look from Jet instantly. Jericho elbowed Quinn just as quickly. "Oof! What!" Quinn cried.

Jericho turned around, facing away from where Jet sat. "Don't freak Fadiyah out," she muttered through gritted teeth.

Quinn cringed, realizing that she'd been about to do just that. "Damn, sorry, didn't think about that," she whispered back to Jericho.

Fortunately, Fadiyah had been so focused on assessing Jet's injuries, she hadn't heard anything that was being said around her. Savanna brought out warm water for Fadiyah to use to clean Jet's leg, after she'd used tweezers to pick rocks and some small pieces of glass from Jet's shin and calf.

After half an hour, Jet had been given a Norco, and sat wrapped up in a blanket, her ankle elevated with an ice pack on it. Fadiyah had decided that the ankle was indeed just sprained, not broken, much to everyone's relief.

Dinner of potato soup and rolls baked in the camper's oven was passed around and everyone ate happily, huddled around the campfire. Within an hour Jet was half asleep in her chair. Jericho and

Quinn got her up and took her into Jericho and Zoey's tent where they'd already set up one of the personal heaters to warm it up. Fadiyah followed to ensure that Jet got settled alright. Once Jet was fully asleep, Fadiyah returned to the group still gathered around the fire.

"She will be alright, her ankle should be better in the next few days, she just will not be hiking anymore on this trip," Fadiyah told them.

"I'm just glad she's okay," Jericho said.

"Same," Tyler agreed. "It's kind of my fault, I was rushing us, trying to get us off that mountain before it got dark." She grimaced. "It gets dark here a lot faster because of all the mountains blocking the sun."

"It's no one's fault," Lyric said. "Accidents happen, it's part of being out in nature."

Everyone nodded, even as Shenin hugged Tyler, knowing that Tyler always blamed herself when things went wrong.

"Well, we didn't get to see any water in Mirror Lake, but we did see a deer and her fawn, so that was great!" Xandy recounted enthusiastically. Shenin pulled out her phone and showed everyone the pictures she'd taken. It was a nice, quiet evening.

The next morning Savanna was surprised to find Lyric still asleep when she woke. Lyric was usually an early riser; it was strange that she wasn't awake already. Figuring that Lyric had overdone it on the hike the day before, she carefully got out of bed so as not to wake her.

After a quick shower, Savanna started coffee in the camper, not sure if she knew how to build a proper fire in the fire ring outside. By 7:30 a.m. Shenin came out of the back bedroom with Aiden. Savanna poured Shenin some coffee and they chatted quietly for another half an hour. Tyler, too, was sleeping in.

"They really wore themselves out, didn't they?" Savanna said, surprised Lyric was still asleep.

"I think they scared the living crap out of themselves," Shenin commented.

"With Jet's accident?"

"With how close they came to losing her."

"I'm sorry?" Savanna queried cautiously.

Shenin took another sip of coffee, grimacing as she did. She didn't realize that Lyric hadn't told Savanna what had happened when Jet had been injured.

"Are you going to explain that?" Savanna asked in a motherly tone.

"Sorry, I assumed Lyric told you," Shenin soothed. "When Jet slipped, they were on a steep part of the trail. There was a drop off that she would have gone over had Jericho not gotten ahead of her and stopped her from getting to that point."

"Oh my God!" Savanna exclaimed, her hand to her throat. "No wonder Lyric didn't tell me, she knew I'd worry."

"Tyler said they didn't really say anything because they didn't want to scare Fadiyah."

"Or the rest of us," Savanna concluded.

"Ty felt so bad, I think that's why she told me."

"Well, Lyric was right, that wasn't anyone's fault." Savanna put her hand on Shenin's arm. "Things do happen. It just really shows us how quickly things can turn."

"That's very true," Shenin agreed.

Savanna heard Lyric moving around in the bedroom, and got up to pour her some coffee. However, when Lyric opened the bedroom door Savanna paused.

"Oh, you look like you don't feel good…" Savanna commented. Lyric sniffed in response, sounding extremely stuffed up. "Oh babe," Savanna soothed, taking Lyric by the shoulders and pushing her back into the bedroom.

Shenin watched and listened with a look of amusement on her face.

"You crawl back into that bed," Savanna ordered. "I'm going to see what I have for a stuffed-up nose."

"But—" Lyric began.

"Don't argue with me, just get back in bed. Now!" Savanna said. "Other than being stuffy, does your head hurt? Does anything else hurt?"

"My whole body hurts, but I don't know if that's because of the hike, or because of what I assume is a cold."

"Okay, so something for a stuffy nose and Motrin, got it," Savanna said. "Stay under those covers, I don't need you catching a chill too."

Walking back out into the living area, Savanna shook her head. "She was feeling fatigued yesterday, I should have known."

"I hear people moving around outside, I'll go let the bois know that someone needs to start a fire," Shenin said, glancing down at Aiden who was fast asleep again. "I'll put him down with Tyler. You go take care of Lyric, I'll come in and start getting stuff ready for breakfast."

"Thank you, Shenin! It's so great to have another mom here to help organize these misfits." Savanna gave Shenin a wink.

Shenin smiled, nodding, thinking how odd it was to be considered one of the "moms." It was definitely strange, but not a bad feeling at all.

Outside, she lived up to that name. Quinn was standing off to the side having her morning smoke, and Jericho was standing there talking with her.

"Okay!" Shenin said, walking toward them. "Lyric has a cold and has been sent back to bed. I need one of you two to get a fire going in that firepit. I'll bring out the stuff for coffee, we'll need two pots. Do either of you know how Jet's doing this morning?"

Quinn and Jericho stared back at the former Air Force security force member in stunned silence. Shenin had sounded like a drill sergeant for a moment.

"Bois! Snap to here!" Shenin ordered.

Quinn and Jericho actually jumped at the tenor of Shenin's voice. Quinn started putting logs in the fire with kindling, and Jericho walked over to Shenin.

"Jet wasn't awake when I left the tent, but I heard her awake in the middle of the night and Fadiyah gave her another Norco, so she might be out for a bit longer this morning."

"But she seemed to be resting comfortably?" Shenin worried.

"Yes, so far."

"Good, thanks." Shenin smiled, realizing that she'd gotten a bit bossy.

"Now, I'll go help Quinn carry out that order." Jericho gave Shenin a wink as she strolled over to the firepit.

Shenin laughed, going back into the camper to get the coffee pots designed for being on a grill. A few minutes later, Xandy and Zoey arrived in the camper to "receive orders." Shenin knew then that she wasn't living down her drill sergeant moment any time soon.

Breakfast was accomplished in short order. Fadiyah had come out telling everyone that Jet was awake and would need help out of the tent. Quinn and Tyler helped get her settled in a chair with some breakfast.

"How are you feeling today?" Xandy asked, as she handed Jet a cup of coffee.

Jet swallowed the bite of eggs she'd just taken, washing it down with coffee, nodding. "A little bit groggy from the meds. Thanks again for having those along, Quinn." She nodded to her friend. "But not too bad. The ankle is obviously still pissed off, but I'll be okay."

"So what do we want to do today?" Quinn asked the group.

"Well, Lyric is sick," Savanna told the group, "so she'll be taking it easy today."

"I vote for staying right around here today," Zoey said.

"I second that motion," Tyler said.

"Same," Xandy said.

"Yup." Jericho nodded.

"I agree," Fadiyah said.

"Sounds unanimous," Shenin said.

They spent the day down by the lake which was only a few yards from their campsite. It was a nice relaxing day for everyone. Lyric even joined them eventually, all bundled up feeling a bit better.

That evening as they made dinner on the campfire, Lyric reminded everyone that they were moving out in the morning.

"It's normally about two hours around to Bodie, but since it's on windy roads, it's likely to take a lot more in the camper. I'm betting more like four hours." She spread the map out on the table and showed them the route she'd highlighted.

"Are you sure you're going to be up to driving?" Tyler asked Lyric.

"I think after a good night's sleep I'll be okay." Lyric nodded. "Jet, are you going to be up to driving? The stang is a manual right?"

"Yeah, but my left ankle is fine, the clutch is a lot harder than the gas. I can put that down no problem." She winked rakishly

"Hey now, some of these roads look a bit wicked, so we need to be alert and stay safe, okay? That includes you, Jet. Let's all get a good night's sleep tonight."

"Got it," Jericho agreed.

"Ten-four," Tyler said.

"Always," Quinn replied.

After dinner and a round of making s'mores, the group sat and talked until nine that evening, then turned in.

The next morning they woke to a soft rain falling in the park. It was cold and damp.

"Well, this sucks," Quinn grumbled as they took down the tent.

"Hopefully it'll lighten up soon," Xandy said.

"Ain't gonna make the roads any less slick," Quinn commented.

"So we'll all slow down even more," Jericho put in, giving Jet a pointed look as she limped by.

"Yeah, yeah…" Jet waved away their looks.

Quinn and Jericho rolled their eyes, shaking their heads at their young friend.

By the time everyone was packed up and breakfast was eaten, the rain had stopped and the sun was coming out.

"Nice, rain just enough to get our shit wet, then go away," Quinn fumed.

"Shhhh," Xandy told her wife. "Don't be a grump."

"Yeah, don't be a grump," Jet, who'd been walking by them, threw in.

"Shut it, you," Quinn tossed back, making Jet simply laugh as she got in her car.

The group was loaded and ready to go. They'd agreed to follow Lyric, so they'd all stay together and ensure no one, "Jet" Jericho had pointed to directly, got too far ahead. Jet was used to being harassed about speeding, but it never bothered her.

The roads were indeed slick as they drove out of the campground. Just pulling out onto State Highway 108 both Jericho and Tyler fishtailed a bit on acceleration due to the road conditions.

"Okay, let's take it really slow and easy here, this shit is slick as ice right now!" Jericho called into her radio.

"Yeah, I barely hit the gas and my ass was all over the place," Tyler added.

"I'll keep us slow," Lyric told the group, still sounding a bit stuffed up.

In the truck, Savanna looked over at Lyric as she set the radio back in its cradle. "Are you sure you're up to this?"

Lyric drew in a deep breath, blowing it out as she nodded slowly. "If I get tired, I'll let you know, I promise."

"You better."

"Yes, ma'am." Lyric winked at her wife. Savanna merely shook her head.

By one that afternoon they'd finally made it to the turn off to US Highway 395, but Lyric was definitely feeling the effects of her cold once again. Savanna insisted they pull off the road so they could rest, recharge, and eat some lunch.

"You," Savanna said, pointing to Lyric who'd just come around the camper, "go in there and lie down. I'll bring you something to eat."

"Yes, ma'am," Lyric said, grinning.

"And take that medicine I gave you this morning!" Savanna called after her.

After Lyric was out of earshot, Savanna looked at the rest of the group. "Would one of you be willing to drive this truck? I'm really worried about Lyric."

"I can do it," Tyler volunteered. "Shen can drive her Challenger.

"I want Lyric to sleep for a bit, I'm just going to have her stay in the trailer."

"Technically, that could be illegal," Jet observed.

Savanna narrowed her eyes dangerously at the younger woman. "Do I look like I care right now?"

"No, ma'am," Jet responded instantly to the threat she sensed, holding up her hands in surrender.

"Now let's get together some lunch so we can eat while the sun is out," Savanna told them.

The sun had been playing peekaboo all day with them. Fortunately, no more rain had fallen. They got back on the road an hour and a half later, after a long, loud discussion with Lyric, where Savanna threatened "all that is holy" on Lyric to get her to stay in the camper and sleep for the next couple of hours.

Unfortunately, the roads didn't become any less windy once on 395, so they still had to take it slow to keep from skidding. There had been a bit more rain that had left the highway slick. So it still took until dark to get to the town of Bridgeport.

"Hey, so I think we should pull in here somewhere, gas up and maybe think about getting a hotel for the night," Tyler said into the radio.

"There's a gas station just down the road, let's hit that," Quinn said.

"Ten-four!" Jet said.

"Got it," Jericho put in.

"Right with ya, babe!" Shenin called.

At the Shell station, everyone pulled off, and started to gas up. Savanna and Shenin went inside.

"Good evening!" the young woman at the cash register called to them.

Savanna and Shenin waved.

"I'm going to see if they have more cold medicine," Savanna told Shenin. "Why don't you see if she knows of anywhere we can stay for the night."

"Got it," Shenin said, smiling.

Shenin made her way up to the register. "Hi," she said, smiling at the girl.

"Is that your Blue Challenger?" the girl asked.

"Yep," Shenin confirmed proudly.

"I love those!" the girl, whose name badge said Jaimie, exclaimed. "Is that another one? That red one? Holy shit!"

"Yeah." Shenin laughed, nodding. "That's my friend Jericho's, that's actually a Hellcat edition."

"Nice!" Jaimie said. "Some nice cars out there."

"Those are all my friends. Even the camper, my wife is currently driving that."

"Your... wife?" Jaimie queried uncertainly.

"Yep," Shenin said, never one to shy away from letting people know she was a lesbian. "Her wife," Shenin said, pointing to Savanna who was walking up at that point, "is in the camper. She has a cold."

"Oh, that sucks." Jaimie looked sympathetic immediately. "I hope she feels better soon," she told Savanna.

"Hoping some of this will help." Savanna held up the cold medicine she'd picked up. "Any luck on a place to stay?" she asked Shenin.

"Oops, hadn't gotten that far." Shenin pressed her lips together, embarrassed.

"It was my fault, I asked her about the cars," Jaimie said, as she started to ring up Savanna's items. "You all need a place to stay?"

"Yes, just for the night." Savanna nodded, smiling as she did.

"Well, probably the best place in town is the Walker River Lodge. It's down the road a half a mile or so on the left."

"Great!" Shenin said.

Savanna paid the bill and headed outside. Shenin lingered for a moment.

"Thank you again, we really appreciate it," Shenin told Jaimie, making a point of being extra nice. She always wanted to leave a good impression on people, because she wanted them to know that gays were just as nice as heterosexual people.

"You're welcome," Jaimie said smiling brightly. "You all seem so nice."

"Oh, we are, just some of us are crazier than others," Shenin said with a wink. As if her statement had conjured her, Jet came limping into the store. "Speaking of crazy…" Shenin murmured.

"Do you have hair gel in here?" Jet asked Jaimie, using her best, most dazzling smile.

"I, uh…" Jaimie stammered, indeed overwhelmed by Jet's blue eyes and very disarming smile, even if she was a woman.

Jet waited, fully aware of the effect she had on women, even straight ones.

"There's, um, something, down that aisle." Jaimie pointed to the aisle one row over from where they were.

"Thank you." Jet pointedly stared into Jaimie's eyes for an extra two seconds, then smiled and limped off.

"Might wanna pick up some ice for your ankle, so your wife can apply it at the hotel!" Shenin called, purposely mentioning Jet's wife. She almost giggled when she saw Jet wince.

"So she's gay too?" Jaimie asked curiously, her tone of voice shifting slightly.

"Yes," Shenin said.

"Wow…" Jaimie said. "I guess, well, I can see that being a good reason to be one."

Shenin laughed at that. Leave it to Jet to convert a girl with one smile.

Jet came back with hair gel and ice, giving Shenin a quelling look, even as Shenin did her best to hide her grin.

When they got back outside, Savanna had already marshaled the troops and everyone was ready to head down to the hotel.

Within a half an hour, five rooms were secured.

"I saw a bar and grill back down the street about a half a block, anyone interested in dinner?" Jericho asked.

"I've been ordered back to bed," Lyric stated.

"I'll pick you up something and bring it back to the room," Savanna told her.

Everyone else agreed to meet up in the lobby of the lodge in an hour. After dinner, everyone retired to their rooms to get a good night's sleep.

In their room, Fadiyah and Jet lay in bed. Jet lay on her back with her foot propped up on a pillow to keep it elevated. Fadiyah lay on her side facing Jet, her head in the hollow of Jet's arm that was wrapped around her.

"How does your ankle feel?" Fadiyah asked, glancing up at Jet.

"It's okay," Jet said. "Still hurts a bit, but not really bad at all." She hugged Fadiyah to her. "I think that's got everything to do with the excellent medical care I received at Dr. Fadiyah's house of no pain."

Fadiyah giggled at the term. "Doctor is it now?"

"Maybe." Jet grinned.

Fadiyah smiled, she liked that Jet thought she could become a doctor someday. She knew her parents would be proud if they could see what she'd done with her life. She grew serious then, wanting to address something with Jet that she'd heard earlier in the day.

"Jet?" she queried softly.

"Hmm?" Jet murmured, glancing down at Fadiyah and realizing that she'd become somber. "What is it, babe?"

"With this accident." Fadiyah gestured to Jet's ankle. "You could have been killed."

"It's just an ankle, babe," Jet soothed.

Fadiyah gave Jet a pointed look. "What happened?"

Jet's lips flattened into a grimace. She had a feeling she knew where this was going. "When we got to the end of the trail and it was time to turn back, we suddenly realized that it was getting darker. So we were hotfooting it back, I slipped and hit the ground." She rushed through the description, hoping that saying it fast would keep Fadiyah from asking too many more questions.

One look at her wife dashed that hope right away. Fadiyah's look was shrewd and Jet knew immediately that Fadiyah had heard the whole story from someone.

Sighing, Jet expounded. "So, yeah, there was a kind of drop off a few feet away." She saw the look of accusation cross Fadiyah's features. "Jericho caught me before I got there. I'm sorry, babe, I just didn't want to freak you out."

Fadiyah closed her eyes to get her emotions under control. Hearing it from Jet versus the partial comments she'd heard over the last couple of days was rather jarring.

"You could have died," she surmised.

"But I didn't," Jet offered lamely.

Fadiyah lay her hand on Jet's chest, over her heart, the look on her face unfocused as if she were looking inward.

"I could have lost you," she whispered, agonized.

She was reliving the day she had lost Jet for a short time, when she'd died in a hospital after being in a horrendous helicopter crash. The doctors had managed to restart Jet's heart, but Fadiyah had been terrified then. She was feeling those same feelings crash through her again, the crushing feeling of sadness, the overwhelming fear of losing someone so precious to her that living on didn't seem possible.

In her need to comfort her wife, Jet carefully turned to face her, taking her in her arms and hugging her close, kissing the side of her head. "You didn't lose me, babe."

"I could have lost everything." Fadiyah shook her head, as if not hearing Jet's words at all. In truth she was still lost in memories and thoughts of what could have happened.

"Babe!" Jet raised her voice to get through to Fadiyah. "You didn't lose me, I'm right here. You wouldn't lose everything. I've made sure you're taken care of for life, Fadi, I would never leave you without a safety net."

Fadiyah raised her eyes to Jet's, nearly wild with her churning emotions. "I have no use of a safety net!" she nearly spat. "I need you, I need you here with me!" She clung to Jet as tears formed in her eyes.

"Oh, honey..." Jet murmured, feeling a stab of guilt for thinking that Fadiyah ever cared about money or security in the way most Americans did.

Fadiyah had lost her entire family in Iraq. She'd lost them one by one, taken by fate and at the hands of an occupying army of terrorists. Jet had saved her from a worse fate than death when she'd come back to Iraq to rescue her in the nick of time. Fadiyah's home had been under attack by ISIS soldiers when Jet, Skyler, and Sebastian had intervened and rescued Fadiyah. They'd been too late to save her father who'd been shot minutes before, or to save her little brother who'd been killed months before, but Fadiyah had been saved. Her fate at the hands of ISIS would have been torture, rape and then murder. She was well aware of that fact and knew without a doubt that Jet had been her savior.

Fadiyah cried in Jet's arms for a few minutes, and Jet did her best to console her. When the younger woman finally calmed, Jet did her best to reassure her.

"I'm not going anywhere, babe, okay? It was just an accident, and I'm okay." Fadiyah simply nodded, her face buried in Jet's shirt. "I'm sorry," Jet said again in futility.

There was no way to really assure her wife that nothing would ever happen to her. Jet was in law enforcement, things happened. In truth, Jet knew that Fadiyah realized that—this had just been an unexpected scare, and it would take time for the memory of that to fade. Jet held her wife far into the night.

"Well, he's definitely a good little traveler," Tyler commented, as Shenin got into bed.

Aiden had fallen asleep in Shenin's arms and was easily settled into the portable bassinet. He'd been an absolute angel on the trip, rarely fussing, doing so usually when he was hungry or needed to be changed. They felt very lucky at that point.

"I'm glad," Shenin said, smiling. "I'm hoping we can do more traveling as he gets older. I'd love to take a trip to Sacramento so my mom can finally meet him."

Things had been so hectic at OES since the helicopter crash that had destroyed their building, Shenin and Tyler hadn't managed to get up to Sacramento to introduce their son in person to his grandmother. They also hadn't been back to Maryland to introduce him to Tyler's parents.

"Maybe early next year," Tyler said. "At least for him to meet my mom and dad. We might be able to introduce him to snow too."

Shenin laughed softly. "Well, that would be an adventure!"

"This one has certainly been a trial," Tyler said.

Shenin grimaced. "Yeah, it definitely hasn't gone the way anyone thought it would."

"Like the cursed trip from Hell."

"Sort of, but I have to say there have been great moments too."

Tyler raised an eyebrow. "Yeah?" she quipped cynically.

"You know…" Shenin chided, poking her wife in the ribs. "Don't be a brat! There have been, we just have to know how to see things."

Still looking doubtful, Tyler quirked her lips in a sardonic grin. "Explain."

"Okay, for instance, when we hiked to Mirror Lake, we were super disappointed that there was no water. But Fadiyah commented that the area itself was beautiful. She pointed out the cliffs glistening in the sun, against such a blue sky. And then seeing that deer and her baby, it was such a precious sight. I think we just need to see the good in things, not just the bad. Didn't you say that the views from the trail were amazing?"

Tyler nodded, obviously seeing where Shenin was going with this. "Yeah, they were, definitely something I've never seen before."

"So that's what we need to take from that day. Not the fact that Jet got hurt, or what could have happened. It didn't happen, and we need to focus on the positive. Because she has good friends who took care of her, she's fine. It also reminds all of us that the future is never guaranteed, so we need to enjoy what we have right now."

Tyler blew her breath out, looking solemn as she nodded again. "You're right, you're very right."

"Good answer, airman." Shenin smiled.

Chapter 4

The next morning, everyone slept in, taking full advantage of the comfortable beds. They had a late breakfast at High Sierra Bakery, then got on the road, headed to Bodie. There were clouds gathering on the mountains to the west, but they hoped the weather would hold at least for the day. The gravel and dirt road to Bodie was far from easy to negotiate. At a number of points, Jet grimaced as her Mustang bottomed out in a huge rut.

"Hope I don't get stuck," she growled into her radio, after yet another run in with a hole.

"My Challenger's not doing much better!" Shenin called.

"Same here!" Jericho chimed in.

"I'm betting there's gonna be shit all over inside the camper when we finally get there!" Lyric put in. The truck's four-wheel drive helped make it easier to get through, but the camper was bouncing all over the place.

As they pulled into the Bodie National Park, the group took in the view of the various houses and buildings still standing there. The town of Bodie had been born when William S. Bodey had discovered gold in the hills north of Mono Lake. It had become a boomtown in 1876 when the Standard Company, a mining company, had discovered gold bearing iron ore in the hills surrounding the town. The boom lasted all of about three years, and then the town declined as other gold deposits were discovered in states like Utah and Arizona.

The 'get rich quick' miners had moved onto better prospects. The invention of a cyanide process to garner more gold and silver from the remnants of the mined ore revived the town for a short while. In 1893, the Standard Company had even built its own hydroelectric plant near Bridgeport to more effectively mine the site. It was one of the first recorded transmission of electricity over a long distance in history.

The town had declined as people left to find a better life. By 1910 the town was down to only about 700 people. By 1920 that number was down to 120. In 1932 a fire ravaged the town, and by the 1940s the Cain family that owned most of the land the town sat on had to hire people to take care of the remaining buildings and keep vandals away. In 1962 the town was labeled a historic site. It isn't known exactly when all of the residents left Bodie, California.

"Wow… this is incredible," Shenin said, as they walked up to the town.

Wooden structures weathered by age and years in the sun were bleached and spotty. It was obvious that many of the buildings were leaning and ready to fall down.

Jericho wandered over to a house identified as the J.S. Cain House and looked in one of the windows. "Well, holy hell," she muttered, "there's still people's stuff in there!"

"What?" Quinn queried, walking over to take a look. "She's right, there's like an old sewing machine, a bed frame."

"Over here there's even a bowl for water still sitting on the dresser!" Lyric called, standing at another window.

"There's chairs and stuff still in the kitchen!" Jet said, from her view.

Xandy looked at the brochure they'd gotten from the self-service station. "It says here that it was found this way. That people left belongings behind."

"Wow, that's creepy," Zoey said, standing next to Jericho.

They walked the rutted, dirt road of the town, wandering from one building to the next. In the school house, they discovered books still on the small desks, a globe that had deteriorated significantly in the sun, even a blackboard that still contained math problems and the announcement for a potluck dinner on October 1. The General Store still had items displayed on the shelves. Bottles and tins lined the shelves, barrels and crates rested on the floor. A crate with the label "Bay Rum" and another label that advertised "Ghirardelli's Ground Chocolate" was proudly displayed on higher shelves. Everything was covered with a thick coating of dust and there was an eerie stillness to the town, like the people had just disappeared.

It was hard not to think back to the late 1800s and wonder what life was like then. There was limited communication to the outside world through the telegraph lines that had been installed in 1877 before the boom, but the town itself was isolated out in the middle of nowhere. Even in 2019 what was left of the town still sat alone far out in the desert.

By mid-afternoon the group took a break in their explorations and climbed into the camper to assess the damage and get some lunch.

"Wow," Savanna commented as she stuck her head in the door of the camper. "Yeah, it's a bit of a mess in here." She climbed inside, surveying the items on the floor.

As Lyric had suspected the camper had bounced hard enough a few times to open cabinets; melamine dishes, pots and pans, and cups were on the floor. The trash can had fallen out of the cabinet so trash was intermixed with the dishes.

"Let's clear some of this away so Vanna and Shenin can get to work on lunch, and we'll get it all put away," Lyric suggested.

They all worked together setting the camper right and resecuring doors to make sure they wouldn't open on the way back out. By the time they were eating lunch, rain had started to fall.

"Oh, this'll make things nice and muddy," Quinn commented as she looked out the window.

"I wanted to take a look at that mill up on the hill," Lyric said, "and I know some of you wanted to check out the cemetery, so I suggest we split the group and do another tour before we head out. I'm hoping this rain will let up soon, but the longer it falls the harder it is going to be to get out of here."

Everyone agreed, deciding that they'd meet back in the parking lot by no later than 3:30, to give them a full hour or so of sunlight to get back out to the main road. The plan was to camp for a couple of days at a campsite further down I-395 and check out a couple of other attractions like Mono Lake with its tufa towers made of mineral buildups in the saline lake.

The Standard Mill was interesting to Lyric because she liked to see how they engineered things back in the 1800s. Jet, Tyler, and Jericho were also interested, so they went with Lyric. Much of the mill's inner workings were still intact, and the bois enjoyed trying to figure out what areas did what in the process of extracting gold and silver from the iron ore.

The rest of the group went to the cemetery set on the other side of town and up the opposite hill from the mill. Shenin had a fascination for old cemeteries that she felt she'd inherited from her mother who also loved them and visited them wherever they went when

Shenin was little. Shenin even had a memory of having an Easter egg hunt in a cemetery in Louisiana, one of her family's rare trips. They encountered tombstones from the late 1800s, some beautifully preserved in white marble, others that were completely unreadable due to deterioration over the years. There was even a tombstone made of wood.

"My mom loves cemeteries," Shenin told Fadiyah who was standing with her reading one of the tombstones. "She says you can almost read a town's story by reading the tombstones."

Fadiyah smiled gently. "Sometimes I believe it is a very sad story."

"Yes, definitely. We were at a cemetery in Sacramento that documented an outbreak of some fever that killed so many children. It was heartbreaking to read the dates and figure out the ages of babies that were only two or three. Some only days old." Shenin looked downcast, her tone reverent even as she kissed the side of Aiden's head. He was, as usual in his carrier, slung around her shoulders.

Drawing in a deep breath, Fadiyah nodded again, understanding the sadness Shenin was talking about, and her respect for the dead that lay before them.

By the time the group from the cemetery made it back to the parking lot it was raining harder. In fact the rain had turned to sleet. Unfortunately, Lyric had the keys to the camper with her, so they were forced to huddle inside Shenin's Charger. Shenin started the car and turned on the heater to warm them all up. With six adults and a baby, it was a cramped half an hour waiting for the bois to get back.

As it turned out, the bois had needed to assist Jet coming down the hill. With the sleet falling heavily as they'd left the mill, they were afraid she would slip again and hurt herself more. So they'd had to take their time and be extremely careful. All four were soaked to the bone by the time they got back to the parking lot.

Everyone got into the camper and Lyric put the slides out so there was enough room for all of them. After a few minutes of cussing and trying to figure out how to use the auxiliary power for the camper, she started the heater, powered by the propane tanks on the front of the trailer. Jericho made a run to the cars armed with jackets so they could get into their trunks and get dry clothes out to change into.

By the time everyone was warm and dry, the sun was setting, and to their horror, the sleet had turned to snow.

"Okay, let's try to get out of here and quick," Lyric said. "Everyone do their best to be safe, but I don't want to be out here too long past dark; the temperatures are already dropping fast."

Lyric led the group back onto the road and things were going fine for a few miles, but then Lyric started to feel the trailer she was towing sliding around.

"Holy show!" Quinn exclaimed as her tires caught a section of icy road that sent the car sliding.

"Jesus!" Jet exclaimed, seeing Quinn's car sliding, and doing her best to steer on the ground that was quickly icing over.

Lyric did her best to press on, making it another ten miles before the camper was sliding dangerously, to the point where she was afraid it would snap the tongue that was hooked to the truck.

"Okay, we gotta stop!" she called into the radio.

Everyone did as she bade. Jericho and Quinn pulled up in front of the truck. Jet and Shenin stopped behind the trailer.

"Yeah, you were swinging pretty wildly there," Jericho told Lyric over the radio.

"I know, I'm worried I'm going to ruin this rig and the trailer if I'm not careful!"

"So what's the plan?" Quinn asked the group.

"Let's get together in the camper and talk options," Lyric said.

Minutes later everyone was gathered in the camper with the snow coming down steadily outside.

"Does anyone have a signal?" Lyric asked. Everyone checked their phones and shook their heads. "Shit, so we can't know how long this snow is going to fall."

"We were sliding around all over the place too, so it wasn't safe for anyone out there," Tyler put in.

"We gotta stop for now, at least," Quinn agreed.

"Maybe we'll get lucky and the snow won't stick, and tomorrow morning we'll get some sun again," Jet said.

Everyone agreed. The rain had been off and on, but had never really gone on continuously and the sun had always come out in between. There was no reason to believe it wouldn't do so again the next day.

"Someone could try to go back to see if any of the park rangers are still around," Zoey offered.

"That parking lot was empty except for us," Jericho observed. "Hell, I think I only saw one park ranger the whole time we were there, and everyone else that we saw was leaving when we had lunch."

"Maybe we should have been smart enough to follow their lead," Savanna commented grimly.

The group took in that thought with varied solemn faces.

"Look," Quinn said, standing up in her urge to comfort her friends, "it'll be fine. We just need to hunker down for the night, and wait it out."

"Okay, but everyone stays in the camper, I don't want anyone freezing out in their cars," Lyric proclaimed.

"Damned right," Quinn agreed heartily.

"Okay, while it's still somewhat light out there, go grab whatever blankets or jackets, clothes you have to keep warm. I'm going to run the heater, but I'm going to set it low so we don't use everything up in one shot."

Tyler, Jericho, and Quinn got ready to go and do as Lyric was suggesting. Jet started to stand up but was stopped by Fadiyah.

"You stay in here, I will go, I do not want you to put too much more pressure on your ankle."

For once, Jet didn't argue.

Minutes later the four came back from the cars, and ducked back inside the camper, loaded down with blankets, jackets and warm clothes.

They all tucked into a hasty meal of reheated soup and rolls; Lyric didn't want to use too much power, not knowing how much was left in the camper's batteries. They all agreed that staying put for the time being was their best bet. Everyone hoped against hope that the snow outside would stop and the sun would be out the next day to warm the area.

They changed topics when things got a little too worrisome as they discussed the "what ifs." Talk turned to Christmas and what everyone had planned.

"Well, we're headed up to Fort Bragg the week before Sable and Gunn's wedding," Shenin said.

"Who gets married on Christmas?" Jet asked. "And why Fort Bragg of all places?"

"My understanding is that Gun really loves the place, she used to go there a lot when she lived in San Francisco. I guess Sable's willing to give her anything she wants at this point." Shenin smiled softly, always enjoying a love story.

"Well, we'll be packing before we head up to Fort Bragg, since us and Wynter leave on tour the next day," Quinn commented. "Thank the gods for BJ's plane to run us up there and back home."

"Yeah, it is pretty nice of BJ to lend us the plane and pilot for that," Lyric said, smiling. "Never thought I'd be able to say I was in a rock star's private jet."

"On the list of things I never thought would happen either." Savanna chuckled, shaking her head in amazement. "We'll probably have Christmas morning with the girls and Ana. What time did they say BJ's plane was leaving?"

"I think we're supposed to be at LAX at like 2 p.m.," Jericho said.

"Plenty of time to have a personal Christmas morning," Zoey commented, laying her head on Jericho's shoulder.

"Absolutely!" Jet smiled, glancing down at Fadiyah.

The group talked for a bit about the upcoming wedding, and Xandy's tour, and other things that came to mind. Before long, Lyric, who'd been pushing it that whole day, started to fade. Savanna noticed and called an end to the evening early.

"Okay, Lyric needs to rest, and I think we all should, who knows what's in store us tomorrow, so let's get a good night's rest tonight."

"Definitely," Jericho agreed, "how do we want to handle sleeping arrangements?"

"Shenin and Tyler, you should take the master bed, that way you can keep Aiden between you for warmth," Savanna said. "Lyric and I can sleep out here on the dining table bed. The rest of you can figure it out. We've got a full bed and two bunk beds in the back room there, and there's the couch that makes up into a bed."

"Fadi and I can do the bunk beds, it'll probably be easier for me to keep my foot elevated and not bumping it if I'm in a single. You okay with that, honey?"

"Of course, you are right," Fadiyah told Jet.

"We can take the couch out here," Jericho said, nodding at Quinn. "If you and Xandy want the bed in the back room there."

Quinn nodded in agreement. "Sounds good."

"Put on your warmest clothes," Lyric told everyone. "I'm going to set the heater really low, so that we don't use up a bunch of propane. I know we're hoping we can get out tomorrow, but if we can't I don't want to run us completely out... does everyone agree?"

"Yep!" Jericho stated.

"Yes," Quinn agreed.

"Sounds smart," Tyler said. Shenin nodded.

"Definitely a good idea," Jet said as Fadiyah nodded as well.

"Put on extra socks and if you have anything to keep your head covered, a hood or a cap, do that as well," Fadiyah told everyone. "You lose your heat from your feet and your head. Keeping them covered will help keep you warm."

"That's my wife, the nurse." Jet smiled proudly as everyone nodded in appreciation for the advice.

"One last thing, the bathroom isn't hooked up to anything, so flushing... erm... solid waste is going to have to be done with a small amount of water. Keep in mind, the water we have is all we have, so take it easy."

Everyone agreed looking a little somber as the impact of what Lyric had just said hit home.

"Good thing Shenin went crazy at that store, huh?" Quinn commented with a crooked grin.

"That's my girl the logistics queen!" Tyler put in proudly, making everyone laugh.

"Alright, let's hit it," Lyric said, as everyone started to secure their bedding and use the bathroom to change.

By the time everyone was ready for bed, the thermostat in the camper read fifty-two degrees. Everyone was already shivering, but they'd done as Fadiyah suggested and made a point of wrapping up and cuddling close.

"You okay up there, babe?" Jet asked a short while after they'd gone to bed.

"I am cold," Fadiyah answered matter-of-factly.

"Do you want to come down here?" Jet asked.

"I do not want to crowd you or hurt your ankle."

"I'm fine, babe, I'd rather we both stay warm," Jet told her. "Come on down here."

Fadiyah did as Jet suggested, bringing her blanket with her. They arranged themselves on the small bunk and found that being together helped a lot more with warmth.

"Do you think he's warm enough?" Tyler asked worriedly, glancing down at Aiden, who seemed thrilled to have his mothers on either side of him.

"Yeah, he's in that blanket sleeper, and he's got your Air Force knit cap on, he should be fine." Shenin smiled, loving that Aiden looked so adorable in Tyler's hat. Of course they'd had to roll it up to keep it from covering his eyes, but it still covered his ears and his neck where the blanket sleeper didn't.

They smiled at each other as Aiden cooed, and reached out to play with Shenin's hair, and then taking a handful of Tyler's curls to mash them together.

"Think he'll ever go to sleep?" Shenin asked.

"At some point."

Shenin bit her lip. "What do you think the odds are of us getting out of here tomorrow?"

Tyler looked speculative, then shrugged. "Hard to say, I didn't even know it snowed over here, I thought this was a desert?"

Shenin shrugged. "I guess we should have checked all of this out a bit more thoroughly."

"Yeah, definitely on the list of things to make sure we do in the future." Tyler grimaced.

"We'll get through this," Shenin assured her wife.

"I know," Tyler said, nodding.

"How are you feeling, love?" Savanna asked Lyric solicitously.

Lyric drew in a deep breath and blew it out slowly. "Like shit, physically, mentally, and emotionally right now."

"You're still blaming yourself, aren't you?" Savanna surmised. "Because this trip didn't go the way we thought it would."

"Who else am I going to blame? This was my idea," Lyric reminded her wife.

"Right, but there are eight other adults that were coming too, none of them knew this would happen either," Savanna pointed out. "Zoey actually suggested Bodie, didn't she?"

Lyric looked considering, then nodded. "True." She sounded far from convinced.

"We all should have done a little more checking," Savanna said. "This isn't all your fault. There's plenty of blame to go around. It is what it is, we'll be fine."

Again, Lyric breathed in deep to try and expel the worry that was gnawing at her. She hadn't expected snow in the desert. In the mountains, yeah maybe, even though it wasn't even fully winter yet, but the desert? Who ever heard of that?

Regardless, she slept fitfully that night, and was awake first thing in the morning.

"Well, son of a bitch…" Tyler muttered, looking out the window in the morning.

"What?" Shenin asked, scooting around a still sleeping Aiden to get to the side of the bed Tyler was on. "Oh…" She grimaced.

There was a blanket of snow on everything as far as the eye could see.

"It doesn't look too deep," Shenin commented.

"'Bout two feet, enough to keep us here for a while."

"Crap."

"Are you seeing this?" Quinn asked as she stared out the back window of the camper.

Jet glanced out the window next to the bunk she and Fadiyah were on. "Oh shit."

"Right?" Quinn queried.

"We're snowed in," Jet told Fadiyah.

"That does not sound good," Fadiyah said.

"That's 'cause it's not, love," Quinn informed her.

The group got out of bed, and Jet helped Quinn fold the bed back in so they could move around easier.

In the main cabin, Lyric already had the door to the camper open and was standing staring at the snow.

"So this should be fun," Quinn commented as she clapped Lyric on the shoulder.

"We are so screwed," Lyric said.

"We'll figure it out," Savanna told her from the stove where she was making pots of coffee for everyone.

Lyric looked over at her wife, and while she admired her optimism in the face of adversity, she also knew that Savanna would never be the one to freak everyone out.

"We need to figure out our options," Jericho said from the couch that was now folded back in.

Jericho nodded, doing her best to quell the feeling of panic that kept wanting to rise up. Shenin and Tyler emerged from the bedroom; Aiden was still asleep.

Once everyone had coffee they started to discuss their situation.

"Does anyone have chains in their cars?" Lyric asked first.

"I live in LA, why would I need chains?" Jet asked.

"Haven't had chains since living in Maryland," Tyler stated.

Jericho and Quinn both shook their heads.

"Does the truck have chains?" Quinn asked Lyric.

"I have no idea," Lyric told her, "but I'm going to go and try to find out when it warms up a little out there."

"Like hell you are! Not with a cold you're not!" Savanna raged.

"I'll go look for chains," Jericho volunteered.

Lyric nodded. "Check behind the seats and that toolbox across the back."

"Got it," Jericho said, pulling on her hiking boots.

"Be careful out there," Zoey cautioned, "we don't need any slips or falls right now."

"I'll be careful," Jericho assured her, as she caught the keys Lyric tossed her.

While Jericho was gone, they discussed other options.

"Can we hike out of here? Quinn asked.

"I think it's like thirty miles to the highway," Lyric told her. "So it would take about ten hours."

"And you would freeze to death in that snow in about two hours," Fadiyah informed them. "Hypothermia will set in probably in less than twenty minutes. Not to mention the likelihood of frostbite. None of us came prepared for snow."

"So, no one is hiking anywhere," Savanna proclaimed in no uncertain terms.

"No cell phone signals, so we can't call out," Jet stated.

"Is there a CB radio in the truck?" Quinn asked.

"No." Tyler shook her head, remembering it from when she'd been driving.

"I guess our walkies won't go out that far, will they?" Shenin asked.

"No," Tyler said, "they're only designed for a few miles. They aren't going to reach anyone thirty miles away."

"And I'm guessing we can't drive the cars in this much snow, right?" Xandy asked.

"We can't even see the road," Tyler said, "and there were rocks and all kind of things out there that we could hit without a road to follow."

"Think they sent snowplows out there?" Savanna asked hopefully. "Maybe for the park?"

"I doubt it," Tyler said, looking apologetic for having to be so negative. "That's a lot of miles to plow when people probably don't come out here when it snows."

"Because other people did research…" Shenin commented rolling her eyes, then she saw the quick look exchanged between Lyric and Savanna and saw Lyric cringe. "I don't mean you, Lyric! I mean us! All of us! We were going on this trip too, we didn't check anything first."

"I'm the dummy that suggested Bodie," Zoey put in with a grimace. "I really didn't know it snowed here."

"I don't think any of us did," Xandy put in. "It's a desert!"

Shenin narrowed her eyes for a long moment as something clicked in her brain. "Wait a minute…" she said, her tone indicating she was reaching for a memory. "That restaurant we had breakfast in yesterday before coming out here, it was called High Sierra Bakery, right?" The others nodded. "This is on the same level as that bakery… Son of a bitch! This is probably high desert! That's totally different! Damn, damn, damn! I should have known this! I'm frigging logistics for dawg's sake!" she raged.

Everyone's faces registered surprise and chagrin and not having realized that either.

"So we're all dumbasses," Jet said. "How do we get out of this?"

Jericho opened the door and everyone looked hopefully toward her, but she shook her head. "Nope, no chains. I did, however, grab the cases of water out of where we shoved them in the front part of the camper, so Quinn can you give me a hand?"

They brought the cases of water inside. The bottles were partially frozen but would likely thaw in the relative warmth inside.

"I also encountered some Sterno containers that will be good for warming things if we need to," Jericho said, putting the small case of Sterno cans on the counter.

"We need to inventory what we have food and water wise," Shenin said, her logistical mind taking over. "We need to figure out what we have, and how we're going to ration things till we can figure out how to get out of here."

The group went through cupboards and pulled out everything there was for food and water. Shenin, in her usual efficient way, counted it up and did some calculations.

"Okay, we've got forty bottles of water, so that's four bottles per person to last us. However long we're out here. I suggest we use the Sterno and a pan to melt some snow for cooking and for the bathroom water we need."

The group nodded. "If things get desperate, we can melt snow for drinking water too, we just have to be careful about it," Lyric put in. "We need to stay away from any contaminants like the cars or anything to collect it."

"Hygiene is important," Shenin put in, "but showers and the like aren't possible. Because Tyler and I are first-time parents taking their baby on a trip we naturally over packed on baby wipes, so we can use some of those for general hygienic purposes. Lyric still has a cold, so we're going to need to use the one cannister of disinfecting wipes we have for trying to keep surfaces clean."

"Hey, I have the makings for antibacterial solution," Savanna commented, looking at the box of bathroom items she'd pulled out from the camper's storage. "There's some aloe gel in here probably to treat sunburn and there's also rubbing alcohol, we mix that it makes a good antibacterial."

"That's great!" Shenin said, nodding. "Okay so everyone should try to use that as often as possible and not touch their face too much. The last thing we need right now is for all of us to get sick."

"I think I'm too late for that," Jericho commented with a grimace. "I've been feeling lousy all morning."

"Babe!" Zoey exclaimed. "Why didn't you let one of us go slogging through the snow?"

Jericho shrugged. "Didn't really think about it."

"You need to get those wet boots and socks off right now," Fadiyah told Jericho. "Get dry pants on too."

"Yes, ma'am." Jericho grinned at being ordered around.

"Come on, I'll help you," Zoey told her, going over to their bag of clothes and starting to pull out items.

The rest of the group looked back at Shenin.

"Now food, we're a little less prepared on. We'll need to stretch what we have, so everyone will be eating smaller portions for the next few days. I'll finally lose those last few pounds of baby weight."

"What's the ultimate plan here?" Jet asked. It's what they all wanted to know.

Shenin took a deep breath, blowing it out slowly, shaking her head. "I'm thinking if worse comes to worse we're going to have to try to hike out of here, but I'd rather not chance that until we have no other choice."

Everyone nodded their heads slowly, each of them thinking about what that meant. By that afternoon, Jericho was running a fever and feeling horrendous. Savanna gave her some of the cold medicine she'd picked up in town, and Zoey took her into the back room so she could rest without being disturbed.

"I think we'd be better off having Jericho stay back there, so she's more or less isolated," Shenin mentioned, just as Lyric began to cough.

"I think we should be back there too," Savanna said, nodding. "Come on, honey, let's get you tucked in."

"I'll get our stuff," Quinn said.

"Can you grab ours too?" Jet asked.

An hour later, Lyric was settled and sleeping, as was Jericho. Both Savanna and Zoey used the antibacterial solution Shenin had mixed up while they were settling their bois. The group spent the rest of the day discussing various options, and keeping an eye on the snow outside. The sun had not come out that day, and a few times it had snowed again. At one point Savanna pulled out the board games that had been stowed in the drawers beneath the dinette.

"We got Monopoly, Scrabble and Yahtzee, and a deck of cards."

"Cards," Quinn indicated, holding her hand up.

"I'm with Quinn," Jet said.

"What are we playing?" Tyler asked.

"Pokey?" Quinn suggested.

"Sounds good." Tyler nodded, as did Jet.

"Who wants to play Monopoly?" Savanna asked.

"I'll play." Shenin moved to sit at the table, as the bois went to sit on the couch.

"Me too," Zoey said, moving over on the horseshoe dinette to give Shenin room.

"Count me in too," Xandy agreed.

Fadiyah looked unsure. "I do not know how to play."

"We'll teach you," Savanna offered.

Over the next few hours, Jet won a number of hands over poker, prompting them to switch to blackjack before Quinn killed her for cheating, which she was sure had to be the case.

Fadiyah became a real estate tycoon on Monopoly, thoroughly enjoying herself in the process.

"I like this game!" she exclaimed, as Shenin had to pay her for landing on Park Place once again.

"Maybe you should have gone into real estate instead of nursing." Zoey smiled as the rest of the girls chuckled.

"I think I should try to start some dinner," Savanna said, glancing at her watch. "I have some leftover vegetables from making the potato soup, so what does everyone say to some chicken noodle soup?"

"Oh, sounds great!" Tyler replied enthusiastically, and everyone else agreed.

"I'll help," Shenin said getting up.

Zoey, Xandy, and Fadiyah busied themselves putting away the game and getting out dishes for the meal. Before long the camper smelled wonderful with the cooking soup. They'd used leftover chicken from one of the previous night's meals, and had preheated the vegetables in the microwave before putting them in the broth to keep from using too much propane to run the stove.

They ate small portions to conserve as much as they could. Zoey and Savanna took soup to Jericho and Lyric.

"How are they?" Shenin asked Savanna when she came back out.

Savanna went directly over to the antibacterial solution, looking back at Shenin. "Lyric seems better. Jericho seems like she's worse. I'm getting a little worried."

"What are her symptoms?" Fadiyah asked, as she dried off dishes from dinner.

"I'll let Zoey answer," Savanna said as Zoey came out of the back bedroom.

"What?" Zoey queried, even as she accepted the bottle of antibacterial solution from Savanna.

"What are Jericho's symptoms?" Shenin repeated.

"She's got a fever, and her head is stuffed up, she says it hurts a lot."

"What did you give her earlier?" Fadiyah asked Savanna.

"This," Savanna said, handing Fadiyah the bottle of cold medicine.

Fadiyah read the ingredients and the indications on the bottle, nodding her head. "The problem might be that this is multi-symptom, and it is better to treat each symptom specifically." When everyone looked at her in confusion, she continued, "This medicine is designed to treat fever, cough, runny nose, and congestion. It has both a decongestant and an antihistamine in it for the runny nose and congestion. The problem is that for some people when those two ingredients are combined, they act against each other. The decongestant breaks up the mucus, but the antihistamine dries it up before it can drain, thus causing the headache."

"What should we do?" Zoey asked.

"The best thing would be steam," Fadiyah said, grimacing as she realized that it wasn't really possible in their current situation. "Does anyone have a decongestant? Something like Sudafed?"

"I think I have some in the car in my glove box," Jet said. "Remember when I kept getting congested from allergies in the summer?"

"Yes, that would be good," Fadiyah said, her mind racing.

"I'll go grab it," Quinn said standing up.

"Thanks!" Jet said, tossing Quinn her keys.

"Also please get the Motrin that we have in the glove box as well," Fadiyah told her. "That will help with the fever."

"Will do." Quinn nodded, pulling on her boots and her jacket.

As Quinn left the camper, a blast of cold air shot through the open door that had everyone shivering.

"I need a bottle of water and some table salt," Fadiyah said. "I do not suppose that this camper has anything like a turkey baster, does it?"

Savanna blinked a couple of times, then turned to look through the drawers and cabinets. "Well, that's scary," Savanna said, as she pulled out a turkey baster.

"We will need to sterilize it, is there bleach?" Fadiyah said, moving to the kitchen area. Savanna pulled a small bottle of bleach out from under the sink. "We can use some heated water and about five percent bleach to sterilize it."

"I'm afraid to ask what you're going to do with that…" Jet commented with a horrified look on her face.

Fadiyah smiled at Jet's expression. "Silly, I am going to use it to rinse Jericho's sinuses so hopefully she can breathe better."

"Instead of the steam," Jet said, nodding. Fadiyah had made her take long, steamy showers whenever she got a head cold. "The solution will rewet the stuff that's dried up in Jericho's head so she can get it out by blowing her nose," she explained to the group.

"Wow," Zoey said sincerely, "thank goodness for our resident nurse. Thank you so much, Fadiyah."

"It is my honor," Fadiyah said, inclining her head.

An hour later after medications and the sinus rinse had been administered Zoey emerged from the bedroom after settling Jericho back in bed.

"She's already feeling better." Zoey smiled happily, relief evident on her face. "Thank you again," she said to Fadiyah.

"I am always happy to help."

That night everyone went to bed in their new locations. The temperatures outside seemed even colder, and the wind had picked up, rocking the camper frequently with heavy gusts. A few times some of them worried the trailer would actually blow over. No one slept well that night.

They woke the next morning to find that a snow drift had piled against the door. No matter how hard they shoved they could not get the door open.

"Well, this isn't good," Quinn said.

"No, it's not," Jet stated. "It looks like the sun is coming out though. If it melts that snow against the door, we could be really stuck in here."

"There's an emergency exit back here," Lyric said from the doorway to the back bedroom. "It doesn't look like the snow is too high here."

A mission was launched to get out through the emergency exit window, and to clear the door. Quinn and Tyler got out and, using a camping shovel Tyler had with her camping supplies in the Challenger, they were able to dig the snow away from the door so it could be opened again. By the time they got back into the camper, however, they were both soaking wet and freezing.

"Okay, let's get them warm," Shenin said, looking at Tyler. "I put some clothes in the bedroom for you. Take off everything and put on the dry stuff."

"Your clothes are in the bathroom," Xandy told Quinn.

"Thank you, love." Quinn nodded as she headed into the bathroom.

"Thanks, babe," Tyler said, leaning over to kiss Shenin on her way to the bedroom.

"How's Jericho doing?" Shenin asked Zoey, who had just emerged from the back bedroom, having helped resecure the emergency exit window so it wouldn't let in the cold air.

Zoey shook her head. "She's coughing a lot now."

"How is her congestion?" Fadiyah asked.

"It was better for a while last night, but today it seems to have moved to her chest." Zoey sounded anxious.

"How is her fever?"

"It's up again. She's really hot."

"We will need to watch her closely. It could still be a cold, but if her cough gets worse and the fever won't stay down, it could be bronchitis or pneumonia."

The seriousness of that statement served to worry everyone.

"We will need to increase her fluid intake," Fadiyah said, all the while knowing their water supply was dwindling. "We may need to start melting snow for water for the rest of us—I do not think it would be good for Jericho to drink anything but bottled water right now. We do not want to take a chance that she will ingest any kind of bacteria from the snow. If we have tea bags we can warm up water and have her drink that with honey to calm her cough."

"I'll go get snow to start melting for the rest of us. Savanna, give me the biggest pan you have." Quinn stood looking serious, she was concerned for her friend.

"Put some garbage bags over your legs and feet so you don't get wet again," Xandy said.

Quinn nodded. "Good idea, who has duct tape?"

Savanna located duct tape in one of the drawers and handed it to Quinn who used it to wrap around her upper thighs to keep the garbage bags up.

"Make sure you go away from the vehicles and don't dig too deep," Shenin reminded Quinn as she stepped outside with the large stock pot Savanna had given her.

"We can add some bleach to the melted snow to sanitize it just to be safe," Tyler put in. She shrugged when everyone looked at her baffled. "They taught us some of this when we were in Iraq. Trust me, it could save your life in a desert."

"She's right, we learned it too," Jet said. "I just don't remember any of it."

When Quinn came back in with the snow, they began melting it on the stove.

"We need an eye dropper," Tyler said.

"There's one for Aiden's Tylenol. We haven't even opened that one yet so it's new," Shenin said.

"Grab it," Tyler told her.

Shenin handed the dropper to Tyler, who glanced over at Savanna. "Any idea how many quarts that stock pot is?"

"Twenty, I think," Savanna answered.

"Okay, so it's four drops of bleach per quart, so we that's five gallons… third of a teaspoon per four gallons, the pot's not all the way full so let's be safe and just do a third of a teaspoon. So that would be a little over a milliliter and a half…" Tyler calculated as she talked, making everyone grin.

When Tyler glowered at all of them for their apparent amusement, Quinn held up her hand. "Do your thing, genius, we're not complaining!"

Tyler narrowed her eyes suspiciously even as she drew out the proper amount of bleach and squirted it into the melting snow.

"So, you just randomly found bleach in the desert?" Quinn asked.

"We carried small bottles of it in our rucksacks," Tyler answered.

"It is really astounding the amount of smart people that are stuck in this camper." Savanna chuckled as she winked at Tyler. "That was really good info, Tyler, thank you."

"Yeah, yeah. Just doing my part." Tyler waved aside the compliment.

That night the wind kicked up again, and unfortunately the heat seemed to shut off. The next morning at first light, Lyric went outside to try to figure out why the heater was no longer working. She found out pretty quickly.

"We're now out of propane," Lyric announced as she came back into the camper. "I need to clear the snow away from the truck so I can start it and charge up the battery. We're going to need to use those personal heaters we bought back in Twain Harte to keep warm now."

"I guess we'll have to microwave whatever we cook," Savanna commented, her mind already turning over what they had that could be microwaved.

"We're going to have to be careful not to run the battery all the way out," Lyric said. "If we kill it completely we're going to be totally screwed."

"How do we know what level it's at?" Quinn asked.

"Handy dandy monitor," Lyric said, walking over to a small panel in the kitchen. She pushed a button and two lights lit up. "So this tells me that the battery right now is fair, which is kind of half full, but that's because we haven't been using it as much as we have the propane. So I'm going to charge them till we get a full charge in there. Then we'll need to keep an eye on these lights to make sure that it doesn't change to low. If it does we'll need to turn the truck on again to charge them up."

"How long will a full charge last?" Jet asked, looking worried.

"Well, I'm assuming the battery is generally in good condition, but I think like a couple of days."

"But if we're running heaters, that's going to eat up that battery faster," Tyler pointed out.

"But we can't not run heaters," Shenin said.

"Right, so we're going to have to be very careful about watching this meter, and recharging the battery using the truck as often as necessary."

"Until you run out of gas," Jet put in.

"Well, fortunately we were smart and gassed up before coming down here to Bodie, so hopefully that won't happen."

"If it does, we'll just have to start syphoning gas from the cars," Jet resolved.

Everyone nodded.

"So, I need help clearing the tailpipe so I don't kill myself with carbon monoxide starting it," Lyric said.

"Are you sure you're up to being out in the cold?" Xandy said, worried.

"I feel pretty good today. I'll be careful not to overdo it," Lyric said, appreciating everyone's concern.

An hour later they had the battery completely charged, and the heaters running to keep the camper warm. Unfortunately, they only had two space heaters, so they decided one would stay pointed toward the back bedroom to keep Jericho warm and the other they'd keep in the front room until it got late, then they'd alternate it between the master bedroom and the main room.

By the next day, Jericho was much worse. Her coughing had gotten really bad and she was having a hard time trying to drink because her cough kept interrupting her.

"Now I'm really worried," Zoey said, pacing as they listened to Jericho go through yet another coughing fit. "Her temperature is up again, and she can't even keep water down because she's coughing so badly. Is there anything else we can do?" The last was asked looking over at Fadiyah.

Fadiyah chewed on her bottom lip in concern. "We need to listen to her lungs," she told them. "I need to make a stethoscope."

"And how do we do that, babe?" Jet asked her wife.

"Do you have a funnel?" Fadiyah asked Savanna.

Savanna searched the cabinets and drawers again, not finding one.

"We can check the outside storage," Lyric suggested. "I thought I saw one when I loaded the water the other day. I figure they probably used it to fill the gas tank a time or two."

"I'll go check," Tyler volunteered, giving Quinn a stern look. "You've been out there a bunch, we don't need you getting sick next." Quinn had gone out for snow a number of times to keep them all hydrated.

Twenty minutes later Tyler returned, looking rather excited.

"Hey, I found the funnel," she said, handing it to Fadiyah, "but I also found this!" She held up her other hand and everyone saw the radio and charging station in her hand.

"If that's just a walkie it's not going to help much," Quinn said.

Tyler handed it to Shenin who looked it over. "No, this isn't a walkie, I think it's a HAM radio!" She turned the nob to turn on the radio, but nothing happened. "Well, it was too much to hope that it was charged." She grinned. "Let's plug it in and get it charged up. Good catch, babe!" She patted Tyler on the arm, smiling.

They plugged the radio in and to everyone's delight the charging light came on.

"Now, does anyone here know anything about HAM radios?" Tyler asked hopefully.

Lyric looked speculative. "I'm betting between the law enforcement and OES staff in here, someone knows some fire and rescue frequencies…"

Shenin's lips twitched. "I have a list of frequencies at the office… for all the good that's going to do me."

"Wait, I at least know LAPD's frequency and their call sign, maybe they can bounce the call to someone over here," Lyric said.

"It's worth a shot," Jet said.

"Fadiyah, what else do you need to make your stethoscope?" Zoey asked, getting back to her biggest concern.

Fadiyah got up from the table, and walked over to the bathroom. She pulled out an empty roll from the toilet paper. "Quinn, what did you do with the duct tape?"

"Here." Quinn handed it to Fadiyah.

They all watched in fascination as she put the toilet paper roll over the funnel's narrow end and, tearing off pieces of duct tape, secured it to the wide part of the funnel. Then she held it up.

"Stethoscope." She smiled and everyone in the group clapped. "Zoey, let us go try this on Jericho."

After a few minutes, Fadiyah and Zoey emerged from the back room.

"Well?" Quinn asked, having been very worried about her friend.

"It is as I feared, it is either pneumonia or bronchitis. She is very sick," Fadiyah pronounced.

"What can we do?" Xandy asked.

"There is nothing I can do, she needs medical attention, an X-ray and a test to determine what it is for sure. Then she will need antibiotics." Fadiyah walked over to Jet, taking her hands, her voice tremulous. "We must get Jericho out of this place as soon as we can, she could die if we do not."

Jet nodded, squeezing Fadiyah's hands gently. "We're working on that, babe, I promise."

It was another long two hours, while Fadiyah did everything she could to help calm Jericho's cough. Each coughing fit shook each of them to the core as they worried. By that time the radio had enough of a charge to try and connect with someone.

"Here goes," Lyric said as she looked at her notes. She'd written down the frequency number she remembered for LAPD and had also noted down what she was going to say. She tapped out the frequency number and found that it was already in the radio. "Should have guessed that, huh?" she said more to herself than to anyone else, since Frank worked with LAPD like her.

She took a deep breath and keyed the mic. "Calling KJC625, LAPD, this is Special Agent Supervisor Falco, DOJ badge number 5692, over."

There was what seemed like an interminable pause before the radio sounded.

"SAS Falco, this is KJC625, LAPD, go ahead, over."

The entire group heaved a huge sigh of relief.

"LAPD we have a medical emergency in Mono County, approximately eighteen miles east of Bodie State Park. We need a relay for medical rescue to Mono County, over."

"Roger SAS Falco, we will relay to Mono medical rescue. What is the number in your party, over?"

"Ten plus one infant, over."

"Roger, SAS Falco, relaying now, over."

There was another pause and then, to their shock, over the radio came a familiar voice.

"SAS Falco, this is Skyler Boché LA Fire and Rescue, where the hell have you been!"

Lyric chuckled, shaking her head. "We've been camping!" she called into the radio, dropping all formality in her relief. "We're done now, come get us!"

Two hours later they all heard the most beautiful sound they'd heard in a long time. The sound of rotor blades cutting the air as a helicopter hovered overhead. Opening the door to the camper they watched as an LA Fire rescue chopper set down in the field. Moments later, Skyler and her team emerged with a backboard and medical bags.

Skyler and her crew were all greeted with hugs.

"Who's hurt?" Skyler asked, getting down to business.

"Jericho is sick, we think she has pneumonia or a bad case of bronchitis," Jet told her friend, gesturing to the back room.

"Okay, let's take a look," Skyler said, gesturing to Jams and her crew to go into the back bedroom. "Does anyone else need medical attention?"

Everyone shook their heads.

"We could use a way out of this field, however," Quinn pointed out.

"We got a snowplow and tow trucks coming." Skyler winked. "Why didn't you guys call in sooner?"

"Just found the radio today!" Tyler said.

Skyler blew her breath out, shaking her head. "Everyone back home has been worried sick about you guys. I was already in the area looking for you, although I was back toward Yosemite, when I got the call."

"LA Fire is paying you to be here?" Shenin asked.

"Uh, no." Skyler rubbed the bridge of her nose. "BJ Sparks is paying me, he wants his 'damned singer back!' Oh and he was worried about the rest of you too."

"Sure he was," Quinn muttered sarcastically.

"Well, Midnight Chevalier was, she was ready to call out the National Guard to find you all," Skyler intimated.

"Wow," Jet exclaimed.

"Well, hell, most of you work for her," Skyler told them. "I'm guessing she doesn't like it when her people suddenly drop off the face of the earth."

"Yeah, well it wasn't intentional, trust me, this has been all bad for most of the time," Lyric said.

"Not all bad," Savanna said. "We learned a lot, and realized we're pretty damned smart when the chips are down."

"We just suck at research!" Shenin laughed. Everyone agreed to that whole heartedly.

Three hours later, Jericho, along with Zoey, had been air lifted back to Los Angeles for treatment. The rest of the group were taken by helicopter to Reno-Tahoe Airport where they were flown by private plane back to Los Angeles. It took some arguing from Quinn and Jet, but the cars were sent back via a car hauler, and the camper was driven back by someone BJ had hired, once chains were installed on the tires.

After a few days in the hospital Jericho was released to finish recuperating at home with the loving care of her fiancée. She had contracted pneumonia, but was healing well, and was in perfect health before Christmas.

It had certainly been an adventurous trip, not one anyone was interested in repeating anytime soon, however. Regardless, Lyric sold her Indian and her Ducati to pay for the camper, determining that she was no longer up for riding a motorcycle.

"It can't be bad all the time," was Lyric's logic on buying the camper.

"Let's hope not," was Savanna's response.

Chapter 5

Christmas Morning, 2019

Zoey woke up the morning of Christmas, once again grateful to be waking up in her warm, comfortable bed, and not in the camper freezing. She wondered absently how long it would take for that feeling to fade. She'd never been through anything like that before in her life, and really hoped she'd never have to go through it again.

Turning over she snuggled against Jericho who was still asleep on her back. Even so, when she felt Zoey move up next to her, Jericho pulled Zoey against her. After a while, Jericho slowly woke up, and leaned down to kiss Zoey's lips.

"Merry Christmas." Zoey smiled up and Jericho.

"Merry Christmas, babe," Jericho murmured, kissing Zoey again.

After a fairly long session of kissing and generally making out, the two got out of bed and showered. The shower took an extra-long time as they made love to the point where the water started to run cold.

"Brrr, okay, no more cold showers, thanks," Jericho said, after hastily rinsing off and jumping out to grab two large fluffy towels. She wrapped Zoey in one and used the other on herself.

Once they were dressed, they went out to the kitchen, and Zoey busied herself with making them coffee.

"You want pancakes this morning?" Jericho asked.

"Oh! Can we have pumpkin ones?"

"We can have anything you want, babe." Jericho winked. "I'll even make you that cookie butter syrup."

"You do love me!" Zoey cried in mock dramatics.

"Why, yes, yes I do." Jericho nodded as she pulled out what she'd need to make pancakes.

Half an hour later they sat at the table enjoying their pancakes and chatting about the trip later that day to Mendocino county.

"I've heard it's really pretty up there on the coast," Zoey was saying. "I can't wait to see it."

"Yeah, I've heard good things about it too. I did hear that it's cold as Hell up there, so let's make sure we're prepared this time, huh?"

"Good plan!" Zoey agreed. "I gotta tell ya, babe," Zoey said, as she took another forkful of pancakes, "you should bottle this syrup, it's so good!"

Jericho had experimented with syrup to accompany pumpkin pancakes, using cookie butter from Biscoff and real maple syrup and warming them in a pan together. It was the perfect complement to the pancakes. Smiling, Jericho thanked her lucky stars yet again that she'd found someone who appreciated every little thing in her life, unlike her ex-wife who'd never been satisfied with anything in hers. Kelly had always wanted more in her life, more money, more trips, a bigger house, a better car, it was never enough. Zoey was the opposite of that, and Jericho loved and appreciated her so much for it.

"Do you want your Christmas present now?" Jericho asked.

"The pancakes weren't it?" Zoey asked, as she licked syrup off her fingers with zeal.

Jericho chuckled. "No, I think you deserve a little more than that for Christmas, babe."

Zoey got out of her chair and climbed onto Jericho's lap facing her, putting her arms around her neck and staring into Jericho's eyes.

"I have you," she said softly. "Why would I ever need anything else?"

Jericho leaned in, capturing Zoey's lips with her own. As she did, she pulled an envelope out of her back pocket and handed it to Zoey.

Zoey took it looking confused. "What's this?"

"Open it," Jericho replied with a grin.

As Zoey opened the envelope, the first thing she saw were plane tickets to South Lake Tahoe in Northern California. Then she looked at the paper behind the tickets.

"Diamond Wedding Package?" Zoey queried.

Jericho nodded. "It's all paid for, we just have to invite people. And you of course get to pick out everything."

"June 14." Zoey beamed. It was their anniversary; they will have been together for four years. "Thank you!" Zoey said, throwing her arms around Jericho's neck.

Jericho hugged Zoey back. She was glad she'd decided to take the bull by the horns. She was afraid that if they didn't make a decisive choice, they'd never get married. The very last thing Jericho wanted was for Zoey to think that she didn't really want to marry her.

"I love you, thank you so much." Zoey had tears in her eyes when they parted.

"I feel like my present is going to be a little less exciting now," Zoey commented as she leaned over to pull a small box out of her purse that hung on the dining room chair. She handed it to Jericho.

Jericho opened the box and nestled inside was a banded ring.

"Oh babe, this is beautiful…" Jericho breathed as she took it out of the box. The ring was a combination of wood bands on either outer edge, with rose gold bands running next to those, and then more wood bands, finished in the center with a multi-colored green band.

"It's Koa wood from Hawaii," Zoey explained, touching the wood bands, "and this is shell in the middle. It just looked like you to me," she said with a shrug.

"I absolutely love it," Jericho said. "But which finger do I wear it on?" she asked slyly.

Zoey gave her a stern look. "On your left ring finger, until I can put a real wedding band on it on June 14!"

Jericho laughed as she slipped the ring on her left ring finger. "I knew that."

"Sure you did," Zoey chided.

Fadiyah found Jet happily sipping her coffee and sitting in the backyard on Christmas morning.

"It is cold out here," Fadiyah told her as she pulled her robe around her closer.

"Nothing's as cold as being out in the middle of nowhere, Fadi," Jet said, extending her hand to her wife, and pulling her down on her lap to wrap her arms around her.

"That is true," Fadiyah agreed.

They sat together quietly, enjoying the peace of the morning.

"So I did a thing…" Jet commented at one point.

Fadiyah glanced down at her wife. "What do you mean a thing?" she asked, always having an issue with Americanisms.

"I did something," Jet clarified. "Technically for Christmas, even though I know you don't celebrate Christmas."

"Christmas is a Christian holiday celebrating the birth of Jesus Christ," Fadiyah recited, "but a Shia Muslim does not believe in Jesus Christ."

"I know…" Jet put in, trying to contain her grin as she watched her wife work through the process of understanding.

"But I am not a true practicing Muslim anymore," Fadiyah stated, lifting her chin slightly. "I am an American."

"Yes, you are." Jet chuckled. "So, I bought you a Christmas present, okay?"

"Okay," Fadiyah confirmed frankly.

"So, go look out front," Jet told her wife.

Fadiyah looked confounded. "You left a present outside? It might rain later, that would ruin the present."

"Then you better get out there and rescue it," Jet said, grinning.

Fadiyah opened the front door to their home and stood staring in shocked silence. A sapphire-blue 2020 Maserati Ghibli S Q4 GranSport sat in the driveway with a huge red-and-green Christmas bow on it.

"This is for you?" Fadiyah asked.

"No, honey, it's for you."

"You are joking."

"I am not joking," Jet told her. "It's super safe, and it has all-wheel drive, so if you get stuck in crazy stuff like snow again…"

"Do not say such things!" Fadiyah warned Jet.

Jet grinned unrepentantly. "Do you like it?"

"It is beautiful, but it is too much, Jet," Fadiyah worried.

"It is not too much, it is just enough for my beautiful wife who starts her new job soon." She hugged Fadiyah from behind, kissing her ear. "I want to know you're safe."

Fadiyah nodded, taking in the car, still unable to believe it was supposed to be hers. In Iraq she would never have been allowed to drive such an ostentatious car. Not that they would have had the money to buy a car anyway. She turned around to hug Jet tightly.

"It is a wonderful gift, Jet, thank you so very much."

"You're welcome."

"Now I will have to get my driver's license."

"There is that…" Jet said, her voice trailing off as she chuckled.

"Merry Christmas!" Cody and McKenna chorused when Savanna opened her and Lyric's front door.

"Merry Christmas!" Savanna replied, hugging them both. "Come in, Ana is terrorizing the presents right now, and your mother is on protection detail."

Cody laughed, shaking her head. "Are Dak and Jaz here yet?"

"Yes, Dakota is out on the back patio on the phone with a 'client,'" Savanna said, using air quotes.

"So important…" Cody muttered, getting elbowed by her wife.

"She's doing good," McKenna told Cody, "let her enjoy her success."

"On Christmas?" Cody asked.

"All the time!" Jazmine said, as she hugged Cody and McKenna. "Cody, go poke at her, I don't think Ana is going to wait much longer."

Cody stuck her head out the back slider. "Come on!" she yelled. Dakota held up a finger, signaling 'one minute.' "It's Christmas, damn it!" Cody yelled then. Dakota changed the finger she was holding up to her middle one, giving Cody a narrowed look. Cody merely laughed and went back inside.

"She gave me a hand gesture," Cody told the group.

"The one finger salute I'm betting," Lyric put in, moving to hug Cody.

"None other," Cody confirmed. "Mom, is there coffee?"

"Of course, Cody, what are we? Uncivilized?" Savanna chuckled.

"Never! Oh, I see bacon!" Cody called from the kitchen.

"Help yourself, did you two not eat yet?" Savanna asked.

"Oh, we ate," McKenna assured her mother-in-law, "but you know Cody, bottomless pit."

"Dakota too." Jazmine rolled her eyes. "It's disgusting! I look at food and gain ten pounds!"

Twenty minutes later everyone was settled around the Christmas tree. They watched as Ana tore through all of her presents, and then happily played with them while the adults opened their gifts. When it was Lyric's turn to open her presents she found that the camping mishap was still ever present in everyone's minds.

The first present Lyric opened was from Dakota and Jazmine. It was a HAM radio.

"I'm told that thing is top of the line," Dakota said, "and I've got you scheduled for a HAM Cram class, so you can get your FCC license."

"A what?" Lyric asked.

"HAM Cram," Dakota repeated slowly. "It's a class where they help you cram to get your license."

"I've heard of these, they have you memorize the answers to all the questions on the test. They won't even show you the wrong answers, because they want you to pass," Cody said, having researched the FCC licensing process too. Neither Cody nor Dakota wanted to take a chance of losing their mothers ever again.

"So I don't actually learn anything, I just learn right answers," Lyric clarified.

"Right." Dakota nodded. "But that doesn't mean you can't study the big-ass manual later."

"Aw," Lyric replied, rolling her eyes.

The next present Lyric opened was from Cody and McKenna—it was a hand crank radio that would also use tiny solar panels to charge cell phones.

"Uh-huh," Lyric said, shaking her head. "I'm sensing a theme this Christmas."

"Yeah, it's the don't-die-in-the-damned-desert-in-the-middle-of-nowhere Christmas," Dakota said with a serious look on her face.

"Yes, dear," Lyric said. While her words were sarcastic, her smile was warm.

The last present was from Savanna. It was a large box, so Dakota and Cody hauled it over to where Lyric sat. Lyric opened it and found a 4550-watt generator.

"That's one of the bigger ones they had," Savanna told Lyric. "If you're serious about this camping thing, I want us to be better prepared for anything."

"Agreed." Lyric nodded. "Thank you, I love it, all of it."

They spent the next hour opening presents and enjoying each other's company, but then Dakota was looking at her watch.

"I gotta go, but I'll be back," she said.

"Dakota…" Cody began.

"She's helping out a friend," Lyric told Cody.

"Oh," Cody replied simply.

"Just don't forget we have to be at LAX by 2!" Savanna called after Dakota as she left the house.

Across town, Xandy and Quinn had finished packing for the trip they were leaving for the next day, as well as their small bags for that afternoon's quick trip to Fort Bragg.

"Ready for Christmas?" Xandy asked Quinn.

"Absolutely!" Quinn said, glancing at her watch.

They went through their stockings first. It was something Xandy insisted on because it had been her family's tradition to open the small gifts in their Christmas stockings.

"Maybe someday we'll have a fireplace mantle to hang them on," Xandy commented as she handed Quinn her stocking that had been hanging on the wall.

The items in the stockings were always small silly items that they'd picked up for each other. When Quinn got to the bottom of her stocking, however, there was a set of old keys.

"Uh, what's this?" Quinn asked, holding up the keys.

Xandy smiled softly. "Go look in the driveway."

Quinn gave her a suspicious look, but got up off the couch and went to the front door. She stood in the open doorway staring at the custom Indian Roadmaster.

"How... where?" Quinn asked, stunned.

"I bought it from Lyric," Xandy said. "She was selling it to get enough for the camper from Hell. I know you've admired it for a while now."

"Aw, babe..." Quinn murmured, taking Xandy in her arms, leaning down to kiss her lips. "I love it, thank you."

Xandy positively beamed, thrilled she'd made Quinn happy.

"Now it's your turn," Quinn said, pulling a small box out of her pocket.

"Uh, you already married me." Xandy eyed the box speculatively.

"I know that." Quinn grinned.

Xandy opened the box, and found herself looking at her own set of keys. She looked quizzically at Quinn as she picked them up.

"Turn around please," Quinn said, making a circling motion with her finger. Xandy did as she was told and Quinn tied on a blindfold.

"Uh, where's this going?" Xandy joked.

"Quiet, you," Quinn said as she pulled the door closed to the house and locked it. She guided Xandy to the garage where she put her in the Charger.

Twenty minutes later, Quinn stopped the car. Xandy had been trying to convince her to tell her where they were going the entire time. As Quinn got out, she nodded to Dakota who sat leaning against her work truck. Quinn opened Xandy's door for her and helped her out, then she walked Xandy through a gateway, and positioned her on the walkway facing her Christmas present.

Quinn took the blindfold off with a flourish. "Merry Christmas!"

Xandy's mouth dropped open at the sight she beheld. Before her stood a beautiful Craftsman home. It had a gorgeous front garden with mature trees and bushes and a carpet of rich green grass. The house itself was a perfect example of a craftsman with the two staunch stone pillars holding up the porch framing.

"Dakota restored this home for us, babe," Quinn told Xandy. "It's ours if you like it."

Xandy drew in a deep breath, blinking rapidly. Then she noticed Dakota standing with them. "You did this? For us?" Xandy asked, tears coming to her eyes.

"Quinn said you've always commented on the craftsman's when you see them. I came across this one." Dakota shrugged. "It needed some love, but as soon as I saw it, I called Quinn. We've been working on it ever since."

"You have?" Xandy asked, looking at Quinn. "How long have you been working on this?"

Quinn glanced at Dakota. "What? About four months now? Do you want to go inside, babe?"

"Oh my God, yes!" Xandy exclaimed.

Dakota walked them up the stairs to the front porch, and Quinn used the keys she'd given Xandy to open the door.

The first thing that hit Xandy was the smell of real wood and polish. Then the beauty of the front room settled over her. It was painted in beautiful calming greens, and the wood framing was painted ivory.

"Oh Quinn…" Xandy whispered. "It has a fireplace! And it's beautiful!"

The fireplace was decorated with antique tiles that held a pattern of rich violet lilies. Xandy walked over and ran her hand reverently over the rich, intricately carved mahogany mantel.

Dakota loved the fact that Xandy appreciated the small details that made up the classic Craftsman style. She clapped Quinn on the back, thinking that they'd done pretty good. Xandy spent the next two hours wandering from room to room, noticing details and being unbelievably happy. Dakota finally had to take her leave before her mothers killed her for abandoning them on Christmas day.

"Xandy, any changes you want, you just let me know, I'll work with you," Dakota assured her, hugging Xandy and shaking hands with Quinn. "We did good," she told Quinn.

"Yes, I believe we did." Quinn smiled warmly.

"Merry Christmas you two!" Dakota stated.

"Merry Christmas!"

New Year's Eve, 2019

The entire group received a message on their phones at the same time on December 29 at 5 p.m. It read: *Spend New Year's with us! Pack a bag for three days, it will be cold. Meet at LAX at 10 a.m. tomorrow morning! Bring your party finest!*

A ten-hour ride on BJ Sparks's private plane later, here they were in Oxford, England at four in the morning. Five stretch limousines had arrived at the small, private airport to whisk them to who knew where.

Every one of their friends was there, except for Wynter, Quinn, and Xandy who were on tour and in London, so everyone assumed that they had been the ones to send the message. Although Remington was among the group, she didn't seem to know what was happening either.

It was hard to make out anything flying by outside the windows of the cars, but they were definitely in the countryside. They didn't seem to be headed into a city of any sort. An hour and a half later, they turned up what appeared to be a private drive.

"Is that a…" Zoey began as her eyes grew wider.

"That's a fuckin' castle!" Jet exclaimed.

"Holy shit, we're going to a castle?" Dakota queried.

"That is definitely what it looks like," Cody said as the cars drew to a stop.

As everyone climbed out of the cars, they were greeted by uniformed staff who ushered them into the castle foyer. The group stood staring in awe at where they were. Off to one side stood an ancient suit of armor, looking as if it were ready to do battle again, or perhaps ride into a joust.

The soaring ceilings were hung with tapestries that had faded with age. The intricately carved, heavy antique furniture was worn from years of polish and use.

"I cannot believe we're in a castle!" Jovina enthused to Catalina.

"This is definitely cool!" Cat agreed.

"How old do you think this is?" Finley asked Kai as she examined the suit of armor.

"I'd say pretty old," Kai commented.

"I have got to film here!" Legend exclaimed, her eyes going over every tiny detail of the foyer.

"Oh lord," Riley said, rolling her eyes.

"Do not put the baby down," Tyler murmured to Shenin urgently. "We can't afford to replace anything he breaks!"

Shenin chuckled, shaking her head.

"Ladies and gentleman," the uniformed butler with the quintessential English accent boomed out, nodding to Sebastian, the only man in the huge group. "Welcome to Thornbury Castle! Built in the early 1500s, this castle served as the honeymoon getaway for King Henry VIII and Ann Boleyn! We welcome you all. Please follow the staff to your rooms for the night. You may break your fast in the dining hall beginning at ten bells, however, the chef will be on hand all day for your dining needs."

"That's ten o'clock, right?" Sebastian asked Kieran who was standing next to him.

"Yes." Kieran smiled, glancing up at Sebastian.

"I'm gonna be dead to the world at that point," Kashena murmured to Sierra. "My brain is so scrambled by the time difference."

"I'm sure we can find something to eat after that too," Sierra assured her wife.

"I cannot believe we're in frigging England!" Erin enthused.

"I know, this is so crazy!" Cassie agreed.

"Get moving you two," Kai told the girls as the woman in the maid's uniform gestured to them.

Everyone moved off in different directions, ever astounded at the more and more ornate parts of the castle as they moved through it. One room had a fireplace big enough to stand in.

"I've only ever seen places like this in the movies!" River told Sinclair.

"It's definitely an incredible place," Sinclair agreed, as she spotted yet another suit of armor with a plethora of swords displayed in a semi-circle on the damask-covered wall behind the armor.

Shenin and Tyler were shown to a room with a fireplace that was already blazing. The room contained a canopied four-poster bed, and even a beautiful bassinet for Aiden right next to the bed. There was also a couch facing the fireplace, an antique vanity and its own bathroom with a clawfoot tub and marble floors.

"I don't even know where to start…" Shenin whispered. "My God this is awesome!"

Tyler laid down on the bed, sighing at how soft the covers were, and how exquisite the mattress felt under her. "I think I've died and gone to Heaven."

"Well move over and let me in!" Shenin said, as she took Aiden out of his snuggly and put him on the bed with Tyler, climbing onto the bed herself. "Wow!" was all she could think of to say.

Skyler and Devin were shown to another room that also had a fireplace with a stone hearth from floor to ceiling. The rest of the walls were lined with a cream damask, and the canopied bed was covered in a seafoam-green damask. Their bathroom also contained a clawfoot tub and incredibly opulent towels and bathrobes for their use.

"Okay, we're moving here," Devin told Skyler.

"Uh, I don't think so," Skyler said grinning. "Not even on your pay!"

"Oh, but it's so pretty!" Devin declared.

"Enjoy it while it lasts, babe!"

In another room, Sebastian, Ashley, and Ben were given a room with not only a four-poster, canopied bed laden with green velvet, but there was a smaller bed with a solid carved wood canopy for Ben. Ben immediately squealed and ran for the small bed, scrambling up on it, using the velvet covered stool that stood at the foot of the bed.

"I'm guessing he's happy," Sebastian commented.

"I'm sorry, I'm busy being dazzled by this room!" Ashley said, trying to look everywhere at once. Their room included a curved alcove with a table and chairs and was lined with windows. "I would bet you there's an incredible view out there."

"Oh yes, those windows overlook one of the gardens, ma'am," the maid told her, smiling brightly.

"Okay, whoever did this for us is definitely on my list of favorite people right now!"

The room Jericho and Zoey were shown to had both of them stunned into silence for a long minute. It was carpeted in rich burgundy, with a fireplace and the largest bed they'd ever seen, carved out of dark wood that covered the bed in a canopy of intricate gold and bronze work. The covers were rich burgundy. Even the ceiling was lined with mahogany scrollwork. Everything about the room screamed opulence on a royal scale. Intricate tapestries hung on the stone walls.

"I could spend all day examining every inch of this room!" Zoey enthused.

"Well, I think you might have the time." Jericho smiled. "Someone has outdone themselves on this one."

"Oh, this is lovely," Savanna stated as they entered the room painted in warm, rich creams. Windows lined curved individual alcove walls, framed in intricate plaster reliefs from floor to ceiling. The area sported two large chairs and was topped by a beautiful valance of silk and rich brown drapes. The bed was draped in a large damask spread, with antique nightstands on either side. "What's out there?" Savanna asked the young man who'd shown them to their room as she pointed to the windows.

"The countryside, ma'am; gardens are to your right, the forest to your left."

"Very nice." Lyric nodded, astounded by everything they'd seen just getting to this point.

Elsewhere Kieran and Memphis were shown to a room that was appointed in cheery yellows and creams. This room, too, had a wood covered canopy, but it was painted white with accents of teal and yellow, including an intricately carved headboard that went from the floor to the top of the bed. The walls were stone, but the wall behind the bed was covered with a gold damask, lending the room a warm, lovely glow. A small fireplace was already warming the room nicely.

"This is so beautiful!" Kieran exclaimed excitedly.

Memphis, who was standing with her hands in her pockets, stared around her in awe. "You can say that again."

Kai and Finley were shown to a room with yet another roaring fire. Their room was darker, with a black carved four poster bed, with a canopy draping of a heavy vine and flower pattern on a cream background. An intricately detailed tapestry of a hunting scene hung above the fireplace, that Kai immediately walked over to examine. Finley watched her with a wistful smile on her face.

"Incredible place, huh?" Finley asked as she walked over, taking Kai's arm into both her hands and holding it fondly.

Kai smiled, inclining her head, taking Finley's hand in hers. "It is definitely fantastic."

"This whole place is fantastic."

"That is very definitely the case," Kai agreed. "Who do you think is behind all of this?"

"My bet would be BJ and Wynter. This seems like their style."

"Mmm." Kai nodded, thinking Finley was likely right.

Kashena, Sierra, and Colby were shown to a room that definitely appealed to their love of nature. The ceiling and walls were lined with rough, hewn beams, and light, natural colors of green and brown. There was a small sitting space separated by wide wooden beams.

"I could get used to this." Kashena grinned.

"Don't!" Sierra said, laughing.

"Sir?" the butler queried looking at Colby.

"Hmm?" Colby replied, still busy being shocked by the entire trip.

"This way, sir." The butler indicated, holding out his arm.

Colby followed the man to a side door, that was two steps down from the rest of the room. Opening the door, the man showed Colby his room, that included a small fireplace as well as his own large four poster bed.

"Holy cow!" he exclaimed, glancing back at his mothers and then giving a banshee yell as he threw himself on the bed.

Sierra and Kashena merely shook their heads, seeing the uniformed butler smile at Colby's childlike excitement.

Up the stone spiral staircase, others were being shown to their rooms, and reacting in much the same way. Before long, however, the castle grew quiet as the group started going to bed, the long day having caught up to them.

"Everyone settled?" Wynter asked, from the mauve velvet-draped bed.

"They are," Remi said, smiling wickedly as she climbed onto the bed, kissing Wynter on the lips.

"Good," Wynter said breathlessly between kisses. "This is going to be great!"

It was noon before most of the group made it to the dining hall. Fortunately, arrangements had been made to have food available all day long. As they wandered into the large hall, food started coming out from the kitchen. Every manner of breakfast and lunch item was placed on the large buffet tables off to the side.

After everyone had gotten food and sat down to eat, Wynter and Remi appeared, standing in front of the massive fireplace at the front of the room.

"Hi everyone!" Wynter called, as everyone quieted. "Tonight being the eve of the New Year, we wanted to get a chance to celebrate with all of you."

"We hope you'll further indulge us by sharing in our wedding nuptials this evening," Remington stated, watching to see when everyone understood what she'd just said.

"Wait, what?" Kai queried.

"You're doing what!" Jet yelled.

Memphis left her seat and ran to Remington to hug her excitedly, and that had everyone laughing and crying at the same time.

"I was hoping you would be my best woman, little one," Remington told Memphis.

"Me?" Memphis queried breathlessly.

"You."

"So totally yes!" Memphis enthused.

"Tonight at 8 p.m.," Wynter said, addressing the rest of the group again, "be dressed in your best and meet us in the courtyard!"

There was howling and applauding as Wynter and Remi started to make the rounds to talk to their friends.

"So who did all of this? You two?" Kai asked.

"BJ," Wynter said. "He said if one of his stars was getting married, he wanted it done right."

"And you knew about this?" Jericho asked, looking at Remington.

"Of course," Remi said smiling.

"Getting a damned good poker face on you." Kai laughed, clapping Remi on the shoulder.

The group spent the day touring the grounds, even getting to take a look at the room where King Henry VIII and Anne Boleyn had stayed. Remi and Wynter were staying in that room.

"This is too much," Quinn said, when she and Xandy, who'd also been in the know about the plan, joined them.

"It's beautiful," Xandy said, admiring the coat of arms on the ceiling.

"Yeah, but we all know how that marriage turned out," Quinn commented, a mischievous glint in her eyes.

"Stop it!" Xandy swatted Quinn on the arm and Quinn danced away laughing.

"I'm not saying anyone will lose their heads here…" Quinn teased.

"Do not make me hurt you, Kavanaugh," Remi told Quinn with narrowed eyes. Wynter just shook her head as the others looked on laughing.

Later that evening, everyone gathered in the foyer that led out to the gardens. When the doors opened, they were all treated to a lovely fairy garden surrounded by a huge white tent with heaters stationed in discreet locations to keep their guests comfortable on the cold winter night. Various trees with green leaves and white bark glistened with hundreds of tiny white lights. Sprays of beautiful colorful flowers adorned the aisle and hung from the sides of the tent. Whoever had designed the wedding had made sure that people would forget they were in England in the winter.

Wynter's mother and Remi's family were there, having flown in early to help with preparations.

Soft music played from hidden speakers, as the scent of flowers wafted through the air. Once everyone was seated, Remi walked out wearing a perfectly cut tuxedo, with a snow-white high-banded collared shirt, and a beautifully hued rainbow tie and cummerbund. Memphis was also dressed in black, but with her accessories in a sapphire blue.

When the music started for the introduction of the bride, everyone stood and turned to look in the direction of the double doors. Remington stood waiting for her bride and was anxious to see her. She had not been allowed to see the dress as was the tradition, but from what she'd heard, it was nothing short of spectacular. When Wynter appeared, everyone in attendance made exclamations at the sight of her, and many stepped into the aisle to get a better look, blocking Remi's view. It made the moment of anticipation last even longer.

When the aisle finally cleared so Wynter could walk down Remington could not believe her eyes.

Wynter's dress had a beautiful bead encrusted bodice that winked and sparkled in the light, but it was the magnificent skirt that grabbed everyone's attention. It was full and white at the top, and the bottom two feet transitioned into a beautiful, delicate rainbow of colors, the hues blending through every color of the rainbow. Everyone would later learn that the dress had been hand airbrushed by an artist in San Diego named Taylor Ann.

Wynter's black hair was worn long and curled into big waves, and included streaks of rainbow colors to go with the dress. Remington didn't think she'd ever seen Wynter look more beautiful, and the look on her face reflected that awe.

"Ou se yon vizyon," Remi whispered to Wynter as she took her hand and gallantly bowed to kiss the back of it. "You are a vision."

"You look awfully handsome too." Wynter smiled brilliantly.

"Shall we proceed?" BJ Sparks asked, dressed splendidly in his tuxedo.

"You seem to be enjoying playing the officiator far too much, good sir," Wynter said, winking at BJ.

"I'm getting good at it, right?" BJ winked back.

The ceremony proceeded to the point of the vows.

"Wynter and Remi have written their own vows," BJ informed the group gathered there.

Wynter smiled up at Remi, her blue eyes sparkling in the dancing fairy lights. "You have been my protector and my friend. You've been an amazement and a worry." She paused, giving Remington a sad look; everyone remembered when Remi had been hurt while deployed two years before. "You've always been strong, you've always been kind and gentle with me, no matter what a brat I was." A chuckle went through the guests, many of them knowing what a brat Wynter could be. "You caught me when I fell… literally and figuratively, and I will always love you for being everything that you are."

Then it was Remi's turn to say her vows. "When we first met, I would have never believed that I would love you so. When I was tasked with protecting you, I was honestly afraid I might kill you myself a few times." She winked at Wynter on that note, again causing a fluttering of laughter. "But when I came to know you, really know you, how could I not love you? Se rezon mwen ye, you are my reason for being." She translated the last for Wynter and the guests.

A number of "awws" and sighs went up from the group.

Shortly after that, Wynter and Remi were pronounced married.

The reception that followed, gave everyone a chance to dance and enjoy themselves. They still had another day in England to enjoy their surroundings.

At midnight, they all toasted to the New Year, with Remi leading the toast.

"May 2020 be a year of joy and happiness to all our friends and family. We love you all!"

Everyone heartily agreed. "Happy New Year!"

You can find more information about the author and other books in the *WeHo* series here:
www.sherrylhancock.com
www.facebook.com/SherrylDHancock
www.vulpine-press.com/we-ho

Also by Sherryl D. Hancock:
The *MidKnight Blue* series. Dive into the world of Midnight Chevalier and as we follow her transformation from gang leader to cop from the very beginning.
www.vulpine-press.com/midknight-blue-series

The *Wild Irish Silence* series. Escape into the world of BJ Sparks and discover how he went from the small-town boy to the world-famous rock star.
www.vulpine-press.com/wild-irish-silence-series